Move Over, Beethoven

Move Over, Beethoven

by *Julia First*

Franklin Watts
New York | London | 1978

Warmest thanks to Bill Jesdale, assistant
principal of Meadowbrook Junior High School,
Oak Hill, Massachusetts, for his open doors,
generous spirit, and terrific faculty.

Library of Congress Cataloging in Publication Data

First, Julia.
  Move over, Beethoven.

  SUMMARY: Aware of her talent, a seventh-
grader thinks she wants to be a concert pianist but
isn't sure she wants to spend all her free time
practicing.
  [1. Musicians—Fiction. 2. Parent and child—Fic-
tion] I. Title.
PZ7. F49875Mo   [Fic]   77-10439
  ISBN 0-531-01472-X

For Ellen Roberts with love
from Laura, Rona, Amy, Sandy, and me.

1 I was so excited that first day, I couldn't eat breakfast on account of nervous stomach cramps.

"Gina, eat." It sounded like a command, but it was just my mother's routine ritual remark. Sometimes my eating gets to be an obsession with her. She's got the idea that a square meal can solve any problem a kid has.

"I'll be OK, Mom." I wasn't sure about that but who was hungry? Today was a sacred event for me. After six years of elementary school—eight years if you count kindergarten and nursery school—I was about to take the next step in the developmental stage of growing up—junior high. How could anybody even swallow?

Mom was dividing her time and attention between the stove and our white enamel table, which, according to my cramps, should have been used for a medical examination. On the front burner of the stove was a pot of wholesome Wheatena in its early stages—definitely not part of my menu but a must for Mom and Sam, the hot-cereal addicts of the family.

Not many kids call their grandfather by his first name, but when you have a mother who calls her own father Sam, it's only natural that the tradition would be carried down through the next generation. A whooshing sound from the upstairs bathroom told us that Sam was in the shower. He'd be leaving in a half hour to attend a lecture at the Main Library on Rare Prints, one of his recent interests. I'd be gone before he'd come down. The day before, when I tried on my new dress, a white blouse with piping to match the blue in my tartan skirt with the oversized safety pin, Sam's appraisal was positive.

"You look pretty enough to stop conversations when you walk by."

Sam never says anything except compliments to me, but I appreciate it just the same.

I don't consider myself pretty—really pretty—but I respect Sam's fair judgment in everything else, so I can believe there's some truth in what he tells me about me. If I had my choice in the whole world of what I'd like to look like—if someone came up to me and said, "Aaah, young maiden, I am zee wizard, zee one who can grant you zee wishes you desire, what shall it beee?"—I might just let him grant me Elizabeth Taylor's eyes, Alice in Wonderland's hair, Joey Heatherton's mouth and, well, I guess I'd quit after that because even with only one of those things, I'd be afraid of the power I'd have. The way it really is, I have short, tight hair, almost the exact color of our neighbor's Irish Setter. And it's not the short, soft, curly, fringe type that's the in-look right now, but the short, frizzy type that if anyone grown up had, she'd get it straightened and use a lot of

Clairol. My eyes are the color that afterward, people aren't sure if they are blue or green. And my lips—well, they're normal enough, but how long it will stay that way with the iron and steel under them that the dentist installed there, is a question. I'll admit that some people have looked at me and said, "What a sensitive face you have, Gina." Frankly, that's not the look I'm interested in, but who knows, maybe the sensitive look will be the rage when I'm sixteen.

Now Mom was urging me, "You'll be OK only if you eat. You need food to think."

"I'll have a big lunch, Mom," I said knowing the size bag she packed for me. "Until noon I'll try to think with less calories."

"A nourishing breakfast is the most important meal of the day." Mom looked me straight in the eye as if her gaze were magically going to cause me to clean my plate. I was afraid she was going to start a lecture on nutrition.

My mother is professionally interested in health. She owns one of those body-building spas with all kinds of exercise rooms, hot and cold dunking pools, and a whole building full of equipment for the express purpose of slimming down overfed persons. Of course, in her mind, I was excluded from that category since she sees me as a frail weakling. She probably tells her clients that I'm a prime example of an underbuilt body.

"Well, be sure you finish everything in your

lunch bag." She gave up trying to cast a spell or force-feed me. "There's a fresh-crop McIntosh apple in there. First of the season."

"OK, Mom." I got up and kissed her good-bye. She patted me on the back and gave me a reassuring "Good luck," and I ran out the door with a sense of oh-boy-I-got-out-of-that-one-easy.

Remi Martin and Lucy Carter were already at the corner waiting for me.

"Gina, I didn't sleep a wink last night. Junior high! I can't believe it's here."

"Just think, Gina, new kids from four elementary school districts—meaning boys!"

"Mmm boys." That was a nice thought.

As of this year, boys were an important new developing fascination in our lives. Remi's father is a psychiatrist and he says that is a healthy, normal response of the female and we have every reason to take his word for it.

"Actually, I'm more interested in their response to us," Remi said. "Daddy was a little vague about that."

"They'll respond all right. Junior high boys are practically MEN." Lucy looked like Columbus must have when he sighted land.

"I'm ready for them." From Remi's expression she could have been inhaling Arpege.

I think Remi has been ready for them since she was five years old.

We were three blocks away from the red-brick-

and-glass structure known as the Brookside Junior High School. To get there we have to pass the Elm Hill Elementary School where we had spent six years of our early childhood. Looking at those little kids going in there gave me a fabulous sensation. Kind of like the first time my mother made her big decision that I didn't need a baby-sitter anymore. When the front door had closed that night and I was alone in the house, I felt like . . . a woman! I just stood there glued to the rug with my head reeling. It was so strange—as if I were a separate person from the one I used to be. It was a little scary too, but that part was very minor. Like today. Part of our excitement was scary, but how could it compare with the rest of it?

The three blocks, including waving, saying "hi" to a million kids, stopping at a couple of corners to exchange descriptions of how we felt, and commenting on how terrific everyone looked, took nine and a half minutes. During the summer, Remi, Lucy, and I had walked that route about ten times so we'd feel like old hands by the time we were ready for the big day. That morning we thought we were closer to heaven than we'd ever been in our entire existence.

It's hard for me to explain what happened after that beautiful moment. From last year as a sixth grader, in the oldest, most respected group of the elementary school, to this year as the youngest, therefore, bottom of the heap in junior high took exactly one and a half minutes. In fact it took the length of time to get from the outside, through the front door to the inside corridor, where the giant-sized eighth and ninth graders were greeting each other in giant-sized voices, pushing all us little kids out of the way. Little kids! As if we were elementary school babies. As they say in my Spanish class, it was like going from *Numero Uno* to *No Tengo Importancia,* in nothing flat. Anybody can figure out what that means even if they take Greek. Believe me, it didn't do one blessed thing for my sense of personal worth.

I looked helplessly at Lucy. Her eyes were sparkling as if she were still on the outside of the door before the shock of junior high realities hit her. Well, I remembered clearly, Lucy is a born optimist—nothing can shake her faith. She'll go through life believing that every slap is a compliment, every failure a success. Some people have that knack, I guess.

I turned to Remi and heard her groaning, which I interpreted as agony from the crush. But when I followed the direction she was looking, I could see that the sounds were ecstasy from her concentrating on a group of boys, each of them at least six feet tall. Somehow, they only made me feel smaller and more insignificant. I thought, maybe I should try and increase my appetite like my mother says. It might make a difference in my self-image.

The space was so tight in that army of bodies,

there was barely enough room for me to let out the deep breath I'd taken as a sign of good intentions for future eating habits. By the time I found my way to my homeroom, 322, I felt as if I'd been squished through a wringer—the wringer treatment you're not supposed to give sweaters, the way they tell you on the labels.

The next hour was spent getting everyone's program straightened out and I finally got to my first class with my head buzzing as if I were in a strange country ten thousand miles from home. Every once in a while, between shrieks from a kid, "What am I supposed to do about B Block?" and a teacher yelling at the top of her lungs, "QUIET!" I reminded myself that this was what I had been waiting for, for six years. Eight, if you count kindergarten and nursery school.

It turned out that Lucy, Remi, and I were going to be together only in gym and Spanish. Last year we had all decided to take Spanish, planning that our adult travels would be concentrated on the largest areas in the world covered by the same foreign language. That would get us to the most countries with the least amount of sweat exerted in preparation. After that first day we were satisfied with our choice. One language was all the sweat the three of us combined felt we had to offer.

We were lucky we did get assigned that class because we never would have believed how bad it was if we hadn't witnessed it simultaneously. Even

Lucy. Our teacher is very nice, but for gosh sakes, you'd think she'd *know* we never spoke Spanish before. She kept jabbering away as if we were native-born Mexicans or Spaniards from Spain, even. I guess we'll catch on later, at least that's the only thing I remember Señora Lopez saying in English that day.

And that gym class. If there's one thing I personally have a strong attitude about, it's privacy. About my own body, that is. Some kids don't mind, like Lucy who never had to wear even a training bra. She went right into the regular Misses' Undergarment Department at age eleven and I'd just as soon not mention the size bra she wears now.

The payoff came toward the end of the period. We were in groups of four when Miss Miller announced, "We are going to have our annual physical fitness test now."

Right away I thought of my mother and wondered if I'd have the stamina.

"You will need only a tape measure for this first test."

I felt a little cautious relief since that didn't sound too much like the rigorousness in my mother's spa. Miss Miller went on to explain that each one of us had to measure her partner in two places. One, around the waist, which I mention first because that doesn't cause me any self-consciousness, and the other place, around the chest. That was what Miss Miller called it. She specifically told us not to measure around the breast. I knew at the instant she used that word that everyone in the class heard me stop breathing. I happen to measure exactly the same around both those circumferences.

Also it didn't help that my partner was not Remi or Lucy who already know my measurements and don't make cracks. My partner, a girl from another school district I'd never met before, who is easily as well endowed as Lucy, just stared with her jaw hanging after she looked at the number on the tape measure and then looked back at me.

She pulled up her jaw. "Gee, I'll bet by the time we have our annual physical fitness test next year, your . . . chest will be bigger."

I pray so, I said to myself and gave her half a smile wondering if she was being sarcastic.

By dismissal time I couldn't get to the front door fast enough and didn't understand how come since I was dragging my feet.

"Hi." I know I had bags under my eyes that weren't there in the morning.

"Hi," Remi answered back. "What a day." She could have meant it either way—exaltation or depression. You couldn't tell from her face, which only looked exhausted.

Lucy didn't say anything, but I thought she had a bewildered look.

We walked a few steps in silence and then Lucy asked us, "What would you say was the best thing that happened?" Leave it to her to put it in that light.

"I think," I began, "I'm not the junior high type because I can't think of one good thing."

"No, seriously," Lucy urged.

"Who's joking? If you asked me the worst thing that happened to me today, I'd say, getting out of bed this morning."

"Gina, why?"

"You mean nothing rattled you?"

"Well, it was kind of busy . . ."

"And confusing," I added.

"There was one kind of hard thing to adjust to," Remi finally admitted. "The whole new language they speak around here."

Lucy nodded. "Spanish."

"No."

"You taking another foreign language?"

"No, unless you'd call using initials instead of whole sentences a foreign language. Do you know what it means if I say SSE in D Block?"

"I wouldn't have known last year," I said. "Or even yesterday. But now I think I broke the code. SSE in D Block means social studies and English at one-ten in the afternoon. Right?"

"Right. I thought Spanish was bad enough."

"I'll tell you the thing that made me feel like a put-down minority group," I moaned. "Seeing those ninth-grade girls. They look like *Playboy* centerfolds with clothes. I'll never make it. No way at all." We passed the Elm Hill Elementary School. "You know what? I think I'll reenroll in the sixth grade."

"Gina," Lucy persisted, "there must have been something good about today."

I made myself think about it. Math, not being my favorite subject, I wouldn't say was good. Science, which I like, wasn't on any of my Blocks for the day. SSE might get good later, but that day it was spent mainly in getting simmered down and getting books passed out. The books did look interesting and the teacher not bad, so I suppose . . .

"The best thing, the very best," Remi said before I could get around to making a positive statement, "are the extracurricula activities. Have you seen the list?"

I had. And that's what had really blackened my day. Even if Brookside Junior High had been a perfect experience, that list would have destroyed me. You could put the name of every single activity on a piece of paper and put the pieces of paper into a hat and whichever one I'd pick out I'd want to do. Which doesn't sound like a tragedy except that for me, any one of them would interfere with my life-style. The life-style I had just been informed by my piano teacher that I had to adopt. I was about to become the only twelve-year-old girl in the second half of the twentieth century in the United

States of America with such restrictions imposed on her that the word *freedom* would be an unknown quantity.

"There are at least four things I want to do," Lucy was getting worked up with enthusiasm. "What about you, Gina?" She turned to me as we got to where the three of us go off in different directions.

"Lucy, there are at least four things I would adore doing too."

"So why aren't you excited?"

"Because of what my piano teacher told me last week."

"What did your piano teacher tell you last week?"

"That it will be impossible for me to get involved in any new developing interests as it will conflict with my new practicing schedule of four hours every day."

2 The trouble was I never should have let on that I had talent in the first place. But it was such an innocent act I couldn't be blamed at the time. It all goes back to when I was in the second grade. That was the year my father died and Mom was looking around for something to do. She needed money and didn't have any training that would make her eligible to inherit my father's practice. He was a dentist. She married him after two years in college majoring in gym. So, after Mom looked over possible jobs and rejected them all, she said, "I'm going into business for myself."

She sold all the electric drills, electric chairs, and everything else my father had used, and put the money into the Evelyn Barlow Physical Fitness Spa.

Of course it didn't get to be that right away. Before that it was the Cosmopolitan Slim-Trim Academy of Health Salon. The lady who owned it was moving to the West Coast and Mom figured she got a real good buy. She took some refresher course and a couple of new ones, put her own name on the salon, and five years of struggle later, has a pretty good thing going.

I used to spend my afternoons there, until I was around nine, so Mom would know where I was and be sure I was getting a healthful snack. I didn't mind because I could bring my friends and we could play in any room that wasn't occupied. The day my big trouble began, I was alone, wandering around watching the ladies stretching, bending, doing push-ups, and flopping all over the place. When I got tired of watching, I went in another room and started fiddling around with the piano. There's an old upright they use to keep time for some of their exercises and nobody was in there at the time.

I'd never touched a piano before. Lessons were things my mother didn't have her mind on then. And to this day I can't tell you how it happened, but my fingers danced over the keyboard as if they'd been on intimate terms with every one of those notes all the years of my life. I wasn't playing any symphony—I mean nothing extreme like that. What I was doing was working out tunes of songs I knew and actually making up accompanying chords with the left hand. Honest, I was so carried away I didn't have any idea of time or place.

I came back to earth when I stopped for a minute and heard a lady's voice saying, "Gina, that's marvelous!"

I turned to the doorway where she was standing. It was Mrs. Allen, one of Mom's clients, in her black leotards. From the expression on her face you'd have thought I'd just composed Beethoven's Ninth. I might have been a little embarrassed, but mostly I was pleased.

Things happened very fast after that. Mrs. Allen ran to the trampoline to get Mom and Mrs. Walcott whose sister is a piano teacher. The three of them ran back to where I was.

"Play it again, Gina," Mrs. Allen said breathlessly.

I did. It was a cinch, but they were so excited you'd think it was an audition and A Star Was Born.

My mother, who, like I said, is obsessive about food—well, she's got an even stronger thing about women being financially independent. Which anyone would agree on, but with Mom it was vital considering what she'd gone through. Anyway, she must have had visions of me and Vladimir Horowitz playing duets and sharing the money equally. Right away she had Mrs. Walcott's sister listen to me, Mom bought an old thirdhand piano, and had Mrs. Harding take me on as a pupil.

After one year, Mrs. Harding felt I needed more advanced lessons with another teacher and a better piano. We traded the piano for a secondhand upright and traded Mrs. Harding for Mrs. Kroengaard. A year and a half later Mrs. Kroengaard thought I was ready for Mr. Sabbatini. He is my present teacher and is not interested in any trades. In fact, he'd like to be my agent and negotiate for my future bookings as a concert artist with the leading symphony orchestras of the world.

In the meantime he tells my mother that I have natural ability, I am perceptive, but if we don't get a baby-grand piano I won't get to first base.

That clinched it with my mother. From then on my daily schedule consisted of six hours of school and two hours of practice and an hour-a-week lesson with Mr. Sabbatini.

It's a funny thing, but Mom never asked me if I wanted to take lessons. I did want to. I was crazy about it. But she never asked me, to find that out. It wasn't that she was ordering me to do it—she's not like that, but she just assumed it was an automatic thing for me to do. That's not the way I look at it though. I don't think of it as automatic. To me it's natural. Like living or breathing, I guess. You see, that's what made it more complicated this year. Playing the piano is no punishment for me. I get tingling sensations just getting ready to touch the keyboard. In fact, it's not just the sounds that I love, but for me it's exciting to make those notes on the page come alive. I could practice ten hours and feel it was ten minutes.

Anyway, we're still using the secondhand upright while Mom shops around. I mean a baby grand is not anything you buy on impulse.

A few weeks back I played a cadence on a Debussy prelude. Mr. Sabbatini closed his eyes, turned his head from left to right and back again about six times like a two-year-old refusing his vegetables. He sighed, "Gina, Gina, a little more dolce." Then he opened his eyes, which were full of sorrow, and his voice was full of anguish. I figured he misjudged me and my whole future was going down the drain. "Of course it's not you—it's that piano . . . that piano." And he looked at it as if it weren't worthy of using in the fireplace. For firewood.

I cleared my throat ready to cheer him up, by reminding him again that Mom was still looking, when his eyes got rid of the sadness and you could have sworn he'd just seen a vision of his patron saint.

"Gina, Gina." He loves to say my name twice —thinks it's more musical that way. "You, with your talent, are going to be playing a Steinway or a Baldwin on the stage of Carnegie Hall, The Royal Albert Hall, the Concert Gebeouw in Amsterdam, everywhere." He raised his eyes to the ceiling as if it were all written there in gold letters.

Well, I'm not belittling talent, mine or anyone else's, but when you get it early it can kind of mess things up for you in important stages of your life —for instance the year you go from elementary sixth to junior high seventh. Or the day you learn you have to increase your practicing, which will give you no time at all for any social life and you know how your mother feels about preparing for the future.

Schizophrenia, that's what I must have, I thought when Remi almost choked on her question. "Four hours a day?!"

Lucy said hopefully, "How about doing the four hours at night, Gina? That would give you time for your personal life in the daytime."

"I don't do the four hours at a stretch, but I have to have the whole afternoon for starts and stops and then save around an hour for the night, too," I explained.

"How about using the night for starts and stops instead?"

"That would get me to bed at midnight and besides, even though my mother has big ambitions for me, she's not that crazy about hearing scales, permutations, harmonics, and contrapuntal subtleties all night long."

"Gee, Gina," Lucy looked at me admiringly, "I don't even know what those words mean, let alone be able to play them."

I could have felt flattered or I could have said, "You're lucky." It didn't matter—whatever I said, it was still rotten cabbage.

"I ought to sign up for the Girls' Issues," I said. "That's number eight on the After-School Program list. I found out that Girls' Issues means Unsolvable Problems of Emotionally Disturbed Girls."

"Aw, Gina, something will come up." Even Lucy strained at sounding encouraging.

"Yuh, sure it will." Remi couldn't manage any convincing enthusiasm.

"Yuh, something," I said.

We got ready to split. "If anything happens, let us know."

"Mm, a miracle," I nodded without any expectations.

I started dragging my feet again. This time it was down Country Road and around the corner to Meadow Street. Number sixteen. My house.

Sam would be home. My grandfather is not your usual senior citizen type. On looks alone you could consider him borderline middle aged. His hair has some gray, but mostly it remembers being black. Also, he has none of the paunchy spread people get late in life. Probably because he's big on active sports. Tennis is his once-a-week regular and any place he has to go under a mile he walks and under five miles he'll bike. I guess my mother came by her phys. ed. naturally.

Sam's favorite outfit is sneakers, a black turtleneck body shirt, and slim, tan cotton pants that he still calls khaki. That's a color left over from World War II. His war, he calls it, to distinguish between the one he fought in and any war that's happened since. He's not a frenetic, flag-waving patriot, but he is high on our country.

"No matter what anybody tries to tell you," he'd say to me, "our brand of freedom is worth any sacrifice to maintain."

"I've no objections," I'd say calmly. Freedom, up to then, was only an abstract idea to me.

Sam came to live with us a year ago. Mom had

been suggesting it for as long as I can remember, but he kept refusing. Then she started insisting.

"Sam, enough is enough. Ma has been gone for eight years now and a person shouldn't live alone—particularly now that you're retired."

Sam's retirement is a joke. I can't imagine anyone unretired who does more work than Sam. He is a dabbler. Or, to use the fancy word for that—a dilettante. That's supposed to mean doing something because it catches your interest at the moment and then you're easily satisfied and you drop it. Well, people that say that don't know my grandfather. Whatever he's doing is for a purpose. For instance, he rents himself out for free to take care of kids if their mother is sick, and he took an orientation course so he can teach blind people how to get around, and I couldn't begin to list the things he gets involved in. His heart is so full of wanting to help, he tries to touch all bases. And he does it without any fanfare.

So when Mom said he should come live with us because he was lonely, I knew Sam would be unimpressed.

"What's wrong with living alone?" he asked her.

"It's too quiet."

"I find it restful."

"If that's a snide remark, I'm ignoring it."

"Nothing snide intended. Strictly direct and to the point. In my one-room efficiency I have privacy, independence, and freedom. What can you offer me that's better?"

She tried another angle. "People will say, 'That's some daughter. Lets her father live in a crummy one-room while she luxuriates in her gorgeous mansion.' "

Sam, of course, could care less about what people think and he knew Mom was making it up anyway. Our house is no gorgeous mansion, either. I guess you'd call the furniture comfortable plain. Some of the things came from great-aunts and great-grandmothers, like the Victorian love seat, making it way over a hundred years old. I don't think Mom has moved a stick of furniture or bought anything new since my father died. She says it gives her a sense of sameness and she likes it that way. Sam says she's living in the past and I think that's why he finally decided to move in—he figured he'd liven things up.

"Well," he said pretending it was a big favor, "I might consider it. Under duress, of course. Until I find something more interesting to do."

It wasn't that Mom needed Sam to help pay any bills that she pleaded with him to live with us, but once I heard her say, "Gina needs a father figure."

Sam had told her then and lots of times since that she ought to get married and each time she's said, "I'm not ready."

I guess she hasn't met anyone yet she cares

enough about must be the reason because I think she has plenty of choices. Frankly, I hadn't felt any lack in my life, but let me tell you that when Sam moved in, father figure or no, having him there was in a special category all by itself.

He might have all kinds of smart, breezy talk with my mother, but between him and me lots of times we don't need any kind of talk at all. I could be mad at something my mother said or at something that happened on the outside, and he only has to give me a soft look or put his hand on my shoulder and it's like someone helped me with a heavy bundle. Or I could feel terrific over some great event and just a shared look puts me up even higher.

The best part of the way it is with me and Sam is that he doesn't treat me with any special deference the way I hear fathers talk to their daughters. Like a girl is supposed to be a china doll. And then again, Sam doesn't act as if he's pretending I'm a boy to make up for a grandson he doesn't have. He treats me like a person. You might say, an equal person.

I got to my front steps not even having to guess whether my grandfather was home or not. Anyone getting within fifty yards of our house on certain occasions knows for sure. The occasions are when Sam is cooking. As I've already said, I don't have an eat-everything-that's-not-nailed-down appetite, but

I bet I would if Sam made the meals all the time. He just does it now and then when he goes on a kitchen binge. It's more than a hobby with him though—it's a labor of love. That's it—an artistic labor of love. For the whole of last year whenever the PTA requested home-baked food for sale or for eating-after-meeting nights, Sam not only brought his stuff in, but he gave out recipes to the lineup of mothers. He joked with Mom about his talent. He told her that was probably the real reason she wanted him living at 16 Meadow Street.

"Naturally," Mom agreed with a straight face.

Sam would laugh good-naturedly and give me a knowing eye. He just said that to let her enjoy herself. You could tell that's what he had in mind. I mean he's always thinking of how the other person feels. Like the time one of our neighbors dropped in and when he was leaving, Sam and I noticed he'd left his hat on a chair. We both reached for it at the same time and then Sam backed away, letting me give it to Mr. Marshall so I'd be the one who'd get Mr. Marshall's thanks.

So now I walked up the steps ready for Sam's empathy and cheer, smelling his luscious fudgy brownies. I could imagine crunching the walnuts between my teeth by the time I opened the screen door.

Nobody leaves their doors unlocked anymore. Or unbolted even. But Sam is trusting. He's got faith in humanity like a member of the clergy, so all the time Sam was with us our door didn't get locked once in the daytime.

I got in the front hall and called out, "Hi, Sam. I'm going to devour at least eight of those brownies." I figured I could hold out telling him my troubles until I'd downed about four.

"OK, sweetheart, eat away, because this is the last batch for a while."

"How come?" I asked, coming into the kitchen. "Chocolate going out of style?"

"Not exactly. The brownie-maker is moving out."

I turned pale. I know I did because I could feel the blood rushing away from my face down to my heart, which began pumping like some industrial machinery.

"Why, Sam, WHY?" My appetite for brownies was gone.

He was washing the pan and said over the running water, "Remember my old pal Charlie Kosta? His wife passed away and he's rattling around in that big old house of his out in Eastwood. He's got a great idea to turn it into an inn and wants me to be the cook." He gave an embarrassed sound that meant he was underrating himself. "Chef, Charlie calls it."

"Sam, Eastwood is about sixty miles away!" I faltered over the words as I realized their significance.

He turned off the faucet and showed me a beautiful smile. I noticed the sagging skin from his jaw to the top of his turtleneck shirt. Jowly folds that even exercise can't hide when you get to be sixty-nine.

"You won't miss me a bit, sweetheart, with all the things you'll be doing. How was the beginning of your junior high career today?"

I'd forgotten that. All I knew was the way I felt that very moment. It was as if the end of the world had stood there and announced itself. So far as I was concerned, if my grandfather was going to leave, the six hours I had just undergone at school were the best hours of my life and in my declining years I would look back on them as a lovely memory.

3 After my grandfather had told me his plan about leaving us, I hadn't bothered answering his question about the beginning of my memorable junior high career, but repeated mine. "Why, Sam? Couldn't you just go and help your friend Charlie and then come back? Do you have to move there?"

"Sweetheart, I have given it a lot of thought and I believe this is the better way."

For the first time in our lifelong relationship I found I couldn't talk it out with him. Maybe his statement coming on top of my bombed-out day was more than I could handle. I hadn't given him a true report about it and for some reason he was satisfied with some things I made up. I had half a brownie and began my four-hour stretch.

I have found that on some difficult occasions losing myself in my music has a real soothing effect. I mean, it seems to me that any time in my future life if I am faced with a rough situation, instead of taking those tranquilizer pills that some people do, I'll sit down and run through one of Chopin's preludes from Opus 28. I think doing that would cure anything.

I was still practicing when my mother came into the house that night.

"Gina, I have located the perfect instrument."
She delivered that statement as if she had discovered gold in the streets. "The perfect instrument after a year's search."

I stopped playing and looked at her numbly.

"What's the matter, Gina? You're not glad about the piano?"

"Mom, Sam says he's going to move out." A piano was the least of my concerns right then.

"Sam says he's going to move out?" she repeated in complete disbelief.

"That's what I said." I wanted her to run into the kitchen on the double and tell Sam she would not allow him to do that under any circumstances.

"Where is he?"

"I am here." Sam walked in the living room wearing his big white butcher's apron with SAM in red letters painted across the front. We gave it to him for his birthday two months before when we had a surprise party for him. I was certain he knew about it, but he never let on and no one ever suspected. That all seemed like fifty-eight years ago. And nine years is the furthest back I remember, so that gives you an idea how old I felt.

"Samuel Parker, what's got into you?" Mom attacked him face-to-face.

"It's time to move on," my grandfather said.

"Time to move on? You sound like an old-time western movie. What kind of talk is that?"

"Ev, it's very simple. Charlie asked me if I'd help him start a new venture and it seems like an interesting challenge."

Mom flopped on the nearest chair. "Doing what?" she asked. It sounded half accusing and half shocked.

"He's got a job as cook," I put in real fast as if he couldn't answer for himself. I was afraid he was going to build up the job to make it seem glamorous and I didn't want Mom thinking it was OK.

"What does Charlie Kosta need you to cook for him for? Aren't frozen dinners good enough for him?" Mom was on my side all right.

Sam told her about the inn.

She leaned forward and looked at her father as if she were memorizing the minute details of his face. "You've got a job here as cook," she said. "Of course I realize you're not getting paid here . . ."

If I was in the mood I'd have told her I thought that was a snide remark.

"The job with Charlie is, for me, strictly a nonprofit venture."

"What's so profitable about a nonprofit venture?" Nonprofit was an expression my mother was prejudiced against.

Sam answered, "Everything but money." Which, of course, was Sam's way of looking at things.

"You're mad." She studied his face some more. "Or bored."

Sam nodded. "A little of each."

Mom looked as if she agreed but didn't want to.

"It's nothing personal, Ev. You know that."

"When are you going?"

So she was accepting it.

"In the morning. Early."

"What's your big rush?"

"Once I made up my mind, I couldn't see any point in dragging it out."

Mom didn't say a word. She just swallowed hard and looked the other way. There was the loudest silence I ever listened to. And the longest.

Finally Sam said, putting his arms around us, "Oh c'mon, I'm not going to another planet. I've made supper, so why don't you girls set the table and let's eat."

He went to the kitchen and Mom and I went in the dining room as if we were finding our way there in the dark. We did a lot of sighing, passing sad looks to each other and some of the dishes got slammed down instead of getting gently placed where they belong.

Like he was adding insult to injury, supper was a Sam Special. Seafood crepe was the main dish.

"Sam," I remembered saying to him after my

first taste of it last year, "you should open a restaurant."

Boy, the things that come back to haunt you.

It was mostly quiet for the whole meal. Our usual give-and-take exchange wasn't working. I watched my mother doing a first-rate job of food picking, so I didn't have to make an effort either. When she served the strawberries Romanoff, I thought she was going to break down and drown the stuff in a flood of her tears.

I'm not sure if I felt worse that night missing my grandfather in advance, or from thinking of the lots of times later on when I would rush home from school to tell him something, forgetting until I got inside the door that he wasn't there anymore.

The dreams I had that night were the kind you get if you have a high fever as a result of food poisoning. I had Mom running off somewhere with her good friend Harry Stephens, leaving me alone in the house with a baby-grand piano, and Brookside Junior High suspending me because I wasn't joining any after-school groups. I was soaking with perspiration when I woke up next morning.

Breakfast was like a memorial service. Mom only gave me a half-hearted, "Gina, eat."

I gave her a half-hearted, "Yuh."

We had already finished when Sam came downstairs. I looked over by the doorway between the living room and front hall and noticed his brown, beat-up leather suitcase. I got a lumpy feeling in the pit of my stomach.

"I'll just have coffee," he said. "I told Charlie I'd be there at nine. It's already late." He gulped down the coffee and Mom and I just stood there watching him as if he were doing some kind of a sleight-of-hand trick that we were trying to see through.

"I've stripped the bed and put everything in the hamper," he said, wiping his mouth on a Happy Birthday paper napkin. We had a few left over from the surprise party.

We walked him out to the hall and he picked up his suitcase.

"Are you taking everything you own in that one bag?" Mom asked him.

He shrugged. "You know I travel light. Now listen here, you two, stop hanging the crepe. This is a better idea than you think."

Mom gave him a combination hard and weepy look. "Sure," she said.

"I'll call you in a couple of days, Ev."

He turned to me. I had to look at him even though what I really wanted to do was run up to my room and hide.

"Gina, I left Charlie's telephone number on your bureau. Call collect, anytime."

Then he left. He closed the front door gently and we could hear the stubborn motor of his jalopy balking about four times while he must have been pumping the accelerator. We heard the engine noise from irritating-loud to fade-out and for ten seconds afterward we both just stared at the door. Then Mom sort of squared her shoulders. It was like she came to grips with facing the situation— she was not going to let it get her. That was probably the way she did it after my father died, I thought. I actually shook myself. I'm thinking about my father dying in the same thought channel as Sam moving out. I've gotta stop this.

"Come get your lunch, Gina."

Mom was walking to the kitchen and I followed.

"I suppose he needs to do that." She was saying it almost to herself. "It's necessary for him." She opened the refrigerator door right away after she said it as if she didn't need any kid's comment to go with it. So I didn't make any.

I personally think the whole thing was no great surprise to her. She knew Sam. She knew he'd be restless just doing occasional cooking for us. The only thing was she just didn't want him to go. Neither did I. But I kept wondering if there wasn't some other reason that made him decide. It seemed such a sudden way to leave.

"Well, how was it yesterday? We didn't get much chance last night to talk about your first day at junior high," Mom was saying in a new stiff-upper-lip voice. She didn't refer to the reason we didn't bring up that subject the night before. "Was it stupendous like you expected?"

How could my mother juggle such a crowd of different things on her mind? There she was with her regular business, her worrying about Sam, her concern over my nourishment, the piano, and my career. Me, I have to settle one worry at a time before I can start working on another one.

I could have said, "Mom, yesterday was the worst day of my life" or "Mom, I'm not going to be a slave to the clock. I will practice only those hours that do not interfere with fun activities that every normal junior high girl does on a daily basis," or "Mom, I'm going to give up the piano."

But I didn't. I said, "Well, it wasn't as great as I expected, but not too bad."

"Every day will get better," she said as if she were Lucy. "You'll see." She handed me my lunch bag. "Oh, Gina," she suddenly got the gold-in-the-streets tone in her voice again, remembering something. "That exquisite instrument. There will be no limits to what you can accomplish on it. They told me it was used for only eight weeks at the Tanglewood Concerts by Renata Corsaro, the foremost woman pianist in the Western Hemisphere. And such a bargain." She was going on like a waterfall. "Only four thousand dollars."

"Four thousand dollars, Mom?" I heard myself say in a wobbly voice.

"Yes, dear, but I can take a couple of years to

pay for it. They'll hold it for one month until I make up my mind." She looked off into space, her eyes glistening.

It was a good thing I didn't sound off about quitting. With all the stress and strain going on, how could I break in on her sensational dreams of my future success?

4 I was quieter than usual on the way to school. My head was humming with a lot of noise though. It was as if there were a dozen or so rooms up there with closed doors and voices hollering to get inside. It was such a jumble I couldn't make out what any one of them was saying and I felt like yelling "Shut up" to them all.

"What's the matter, Gina, you've hardly said a word," Remi looked at me and frowned.

"I have a terrible headache." It was no lie.

"Are you OK?"

"Yuh, I guess I didn't sleep too well."

"I bet today is going to be the exact opposite of yesterday," Lucy was her usual cheerful self.

The exact opposite of terrible is wonderful, I reasoned, and already today is worse than terrible, so Lucy is wrong.

Fortunately we kept meeting kids and the three of us expanded to about seven, so I didn't have to fake any conversation I didn't feel. With a gang like that nobody noticed that I wasn't doing much talking.

Lucy turned out to be half right. I had science in A Block, which means first thing in the morning. Mr. Stearns has a great sense of humor and started us right in on chemistry. If my career in music weren't predetermined, I'd consider one in the physical sciences.

And then Señora Lopez went over the same material that she did the day before, which made *buenos dias, gracias,* and *hasta luego* have a lot more sense.

In SSE we started reading *Sucker,* a Carson McCullers short story that was so good I got close to crying for those characters. Maybe if I didn't consider chemistry I might think about being a writer. I mean it's really something to be able to get people worked up like that author did. Maybe it was because anything sad reminded me of Sam.

But the good part of the day ended right there. I got cheated out of pizza at lunch. Not that I can blame my mother for that. Had I known it was pizza day, I wouldn't have brought a bag lunch from home.

Remi and I have the same lunch block and I think it's going to take the whole three years in junior high to get used to that zoo they call the cafeteria. If anyone at the Elm Hill acted the way most of those Brookside kids do, they'd throw them out pronto. It's mostly the boys who do things like flip mashed potatoes off their forks to see how far away it lands. And the screaming! You could send a rocket to outer space in that room around noontime and no one would separate the blast-off sound from the conversation.

Remi stuck her hands up to her ears when we walked in and we just looked at each other helplessly. It's not that we're so affected by noise; there just wasn't a familiar face anywhere. When you're outnumbered like that, I think you're more sensitive.

Remi was stuck too with bringing her lunch and we had to make a very difficult moral decision when we got that gorgeous whiff of pizza.

"What'll we do?"

"Eat the pizza."

"My mother will kill me if I bring home her lunch uneaten."

"Then throw it."

I looked at my egg-mush sandwich. My mother's favorite nutrition builder. Remi opened hers. Tuna. She raised an eyebrow, "Oh well."

We both felt very noble as we resisted the powerful temptation of that cheese, tomato, oregano aroma. Next week we'd remember.

The second item that ruined a halfway decent morning was after E Block, the end of the day.

"Before we go home let's see what clubs and things are available to sign up for." Jody, one of the other girls from our old sixth-grade class, made that terrific suggestion.

I said, knowing it was a pure lie, "I don't think there's much they've posted yet."

"Yuh, why don't we wait for a week or so," Remi added and I gave her a thank-you look.

"They're already posted. I've seen it up there. Also I heard they have a Thanksgiving Dance in the gym the Saturday before Thanksgiving. Isn't that divine?"

"What boy would ask a seventh-grade girl?" Remi demanded of Jody. "And if you mean go with other girls, I will not."

"It could happen!" Jody had more confidence than good sense, I thought. I had as much chance of being invited as I had of paying for the piano out of my allowance.

Lucy was still trying to avoid looking at the bulletin board, for my sake. "There'll probably be a million kids standing there. We'll never get close to it."

"Well, let's see," Jody insisted.

We had no alternative, so we walked over to the wall by the front entrance. *After-School Activity Groups* was the sign slapped full width across the huge cork board on the wall beside the auditorium door. Right under that *Join Now!* was printed like a demand. Then there was a list of categories such as Language Clubs, Theater Arts, Sports, with details about hours and places to meet.

I didn't read all the columns because I didn't see any reason why I should torture myself again. I might find something I couldn't live without and then what?

When Remi saw my stone-face expression she said, "What do you think, Gina? Can you shorten your practicing time?"

I shook my head.

"By only one measly hour?"

"I'll talk to you about it later," I said it low so Jody wouldn't hear and Remi would understand it was a private matter between her, Lucy, and me.

You'd have thought I was involved with the underworld of crime the way I wanted to keep my personal, after-school activity quiet. That's what made it so dumb. I mean, here I was doing a perfectly legitimate thing—the kind that lots of mothers encourage their children to do. In fact, Karen Benson's mother has been holding me up to her for years as some kind of a paragon. I found that out when Karen told me one time last year, "If I didn't like you, Gina Barlow, I'd absolutely detest you."

"What's that supposed to mean?" I asked her.

"My mother," she answered as if that were a complete explanation.

I waited for more.

"My mother," she repeated with a snarl in her voice, "keeps calling you a paragon of the community the way you do well in school, excel at the piano, and are such a nice girl."

"Did she say I was gorgeous?"

"No."

"See. So what are you jealous about?"

"I'm not jealous. Just annoyed. Why does she have to throw up to me that you're a model of perfection?"

"Well, some of us have it, Karen." I pretended superiority.

But now, a year later, I'd have sold my paragon qualities for a nickel, or even given them away if I could be less talented and have a mother who would have been satisfied for me to be a fun-loving idiot.

"What's going on?" Remi asked me as soon as the three of us were alone at the corner of Country Road. "You seemed very mysterious."

"The end of the world," I said. I made some kind of a hopeless sound. "My mother is planning on spending practically a year's income on a baby grand, so how can I cut down my practicing by even five minutes?"

"That's blackmail," Remi cried out.

"Oh, Gina." Lucy sounded sympathetic.

"She doesn't mean it as blackmail," I said, "but just the same I can't do anything about it."

"Sure you can," Remi fairly snapped. "Tell her you're happy with your old piano."

"Oh that *is* a piece of junk, Remi. I couldn't tell her that."

"Tell her it's not right for her to spend the money."

I sighed. "I'll try that, Lucy. But she's not planning to pay for it all at once."

"Well, try."

"OK, I'll try."

Somewhere in the inside middle of me, I got a small ache. How I wish some benevolent millionaire would donate his baby grand to us. The feel and the sound of the "perfect instrument" would sure be nice.

When I left them I realized I hadn't said anything about Sam. It was as if I had discarded him like leaving old clothes at the pickup center while I thought about things that affected me for my own personal pleasure. Well, Sam's leaving sure affected me personally. Such as coming home to an empty house.

I sat on my old piano stool and wondered if the Baldwin people threw in a new seat with the four-thousand-dollar deal. I hoped not. I liked my old, familiar, adjustable one instead of those long rectangular benches that look like coffins when you lift up the whole top to get to the music that's stored inside. I took a snack break after the first half hour. I thought of Sam's butterscotch chip cookies and how he used to bring them over to the piano.

I also thought about how I knew I had always loved Sam, but the day I found out a special reason for it was when Lucy, Remi, and I made our first dry run to Brookside last June. When I had come home I started to practice and I had this opalescent glow in my eyes. Sam noticed and said, "I know the feeling."

I wasn't sure at the moment whether the glow was from my anticipations about junior high or the second symphonic poem of Liszt that I was working on. I wasn't even sure which one Sam was referring to, so I only nodded and let the joy stay wherever it belonged. But then when he went on and said, "It's very important, isn't it, to have something you feel very deeply about," I stopped right in the middle of a diminished seventh chord and focused my glow on him.

"Lots of people don't, you know. Feel deeply, that is."

I knew he didn't mean himself or Mom because there were two people who sure had strong feelings.

He was standing as upright as the old piano, with his hands in his pockets and if I never before thought eyes could talk, I sure learned it then. It's a universal language, I think, like music.

"Lots of people do things and get no real satisfaction from it. You're lucky and so am I," he said it like he wanted me to remember it.

I'm not saying those were earth-shaking words, but it got to me and made me think. I looked at him in a way that I hadn't up to then. Like when you look at a picture, maybe an oil painting and you have to stand away from it to see what more you can read in it than you did when you stood close up.

So then before he got heavy and philosophical, he grinned and added, "Not bad to be emotionally involved in something you'd give more than two cents for, right?"

"Right," I agreed softly.

"Would you give more than two cents for playing music?"

"Course."

"How much? Your whole life's savings?"

"Not *all* my life's savings." I shook my head very soberly.

He nodded in approval. "That's a smart girl."

Now, three months later my fists came down on the keys and made a thunderchord.

After another half hour when I'd been concentrating on everything but Etude no. 22, I got up and walked around the living room a couple of times like they walk horses to cool them off when they're all sweated up after a race. I sighed and said, "darn, darn, darn" five or six times, went back to the piano, and didn't do much more than plunk until Mom came home. Maybe I should have played Chopin's prelude from Opus 28.

Mom came in with the same kind of pep and enthusiasm that she did the day before. I envied her ability to put problems in a faraway corner of her mind.

"Hello, honey. I just picked up a barbecued chicken and all the fixings at the Upper Falls Supermarket. I'm starved, let's eat right away and then figure out the best spot to put the piano."

"Oh, you decided definitely?"

"Well, just in case I do."

She left me breathless even though the energy that was getting used was all hers. Well, that sure wasn't the moment to discuss canceling the new purchase. We ate the chicken and fixings and it no way came near Sam's. Or Mom's. She's a pretty good cook in her own right when she wants to take the time.

She kept bubbling over with statements like, "Now you know, Gina, we can't put the piano in the alcove where the upright is—a baby grand needs breathing space." She put her hand on her chest as if she were breathing for a human piano. "And," she went on, "we have to keep it out of a draft, away from glass walls, windows, air-conditioners, radiators, or damp rooms."

I looked at her positively unbelieving. She sounded as if she were talking about a sick newborn infant, and we didn't have any glass walls or air-conditioners in the house anyway. I couldn't even ask her where she got all that crazy information, but she supplied it unasked.

"Mr. Armstrong from the piano outlet stopped by the spa today and gave me a handbook on the care of fine pianos. You should read it, Gina, it's very informative."

I could tell that, and half expected her to say the care and feeding of baby pianos. I wondered how she'd behave if we were getting a concert grand instead. By the time we were through eating and doing the dishes, Mom was giving me the benefit of what must have been chapter two in the handbook.

"Fortunately, we'll have it delivered before the winter, so we won't have any problems with the room temperature. But if it's a cool day, we'll have to put the heat on to let the instrument adjust to its new environment."

"Mom," my voice sounded squeaky, "that's a lot of money to spend."

She was just closing the lazy Susan under the counter where she keeps the pots. She stood up and gave me one of those melting looks. The kind that has love written all over it. "Gina," the tone of her voice matched the expression on her face, "you are a sweetheart. But, honey, you know it's an investment—it's for your career."

Guilt is not what I felt. If the word for what I felt has been invented, I haven't come across it yet. What made it worse was that my mother was doing all this out of the kindness of her heart. She believed in me. And what made it double worse was that I could go crazy with happiness having an honest-to-goodness, personal baby grand to play.

"But, Mom," I tried weakly, "M—maybe I'm not—that good."

It was almost the last straw when she bent over and kissed me. "Talent you have, baby, and talent must be nurtured and challenged and given opportunity for growth."

That had to be chapter three in the *Handbook to Sell Fine Pianos*. There was a lot I could have told her at that point. Later, when I went upstairs to my room, I took out the piece of paper from my drawer with Sam's telephone number on it. Mom had the TV on, so she didn't hear anything else. I went into what's been used for a spare room, an upstairs family room, or, last year, Sam's room. There's a phone in there. Very carefully I dialed the number Sam had left for me.

"She's so happy about what she's doing for me, I *couldn't* tell her I wanted to join some school clubs, Sam."

Through sixty miles worth of telephone wire I could feel Sam's acute sympathy. "She has to be told, of course, but we can't go in with a club, can we?"

I let him go on.

"When we want to get someone to listen, we have to be subtle, don't you think?"

"I s'pose, but how?"

"Well, give me a little time to work on that, Gina. OK? I want to let it incubate in my mind for a while."

He didn't need any mileage between us to hear my sigh. I had faith in him, but I wanted everything to be settled now!

"Listen, I don't want you to worry. You're going to be your own woman same as your mother. Same as I'm my own man—it runs in the family. Now you hang on to that, kiddy."

"How long do I hang, Sam?"

"Not long, I'll work on that too. I'll be in touch. Bye, now."

"Bye."

I thought about what I was supposed to hang

on to. My sterling character and that I belonged to a courageous, independent-type family. One day I was going to run my own show. That was great. Only trouble was, what about the rocky road on the way? Growing up is not an easy thing to do. My mother, a woman with fanatical faith in her daughter's successful future, willing to sacrifice every cent to make it happen and me, the daughter who wasn't sure.

5 Then on Monday a new complication entered my life. That was the day I met Joshua. Joshua is Joshua Jackson, an eighth-grade boy, and I didn't exactly meet him with any formal introduction. Or even informal. What happened was that on that Monday Remi was absent on account of a ninety-nine-degree temperature that her mother was sure was mononucleosis. Of course it turned out to be nothing and lasted only twenty-four hours, but it made me have lunch with nobody. Not that I couldn't have eaten with some kids from my class, but it didn't work out that way. After we were dismissed from math, just before lunch, I had to go to my locker for the sandwich I left there, and by the time I got to the cafeteria, I didn't see anybody I knew.

The tables run almost the full length of the gigantic room and mostly kids in the same grade sit together. There was one vacant seat near where I was standing and I took it. The minute I unwrapped my egg mush, I knew I'd made a mistake. It was a totally eighth-grade table, practically all boys.

Not that they had lost their fascination for me, but me alone surrounded by that throng was kind of staggering. When it was crystal clear that my presence had no effect on them whatsoever, even as a means of getting salt passed back and forth, I got unstaggered to the point of getting inferiority symptoms and decided I'd eat fast and get out of there.

Some of the boys were going through their regular routine of tossing food around, grabbing and poking each other, yelling, and in general having a good time. The one on my left, who was Joshua, did a fair share of the poking and yelling, but he didn't throw any food, which put him in a good light by comparison. I didn't look at him, at first, and the conversation didn't interest me.

"Hey, Josh, you betting on the football game Saturday?"

"No. If I can't be around to watch the game I'm not betting on it. Eddie's a big spender. He'll bet with you."

The boy who must have been Eddie said, "Miami is too great a risk. I'm not betting."

Of all the subjects in the world . . . if my mouth weren't full of food I could have yawned with boredom.

"Why aren't you watching the game, Josh?"

"They've scheduled a special rehearsal for Saturday afternoon that will not only kill that day, but we'll be staying over my uncle's until Sunday. Which means we'll be driving home and I won't get to see Sunday's game on TV either."

"That's a drag, Josh."

I wondered what he was rehearsing for and where he had to go to do it.

"You have to give up a lot of stuff, don't you?"

"Oh, well." From his voice I could tell that Joshua minimized his sacrifices. More than I seemed to be doing. "All for my art, you know." He made an easy smile.

I saw that out of the corner of my eye since I didn't feel ready to look at him eyeball to eyeball. Out of the corner, though, I could see he had even teeth. Some kids are sure lucky. Good straight teeth you can look at without braces, which are like stop signs for people who have them—like me. That easy smile of his made you feel you had to smile right back. But he wasn't looking at me so I didn't have to.

"Hey, do you think someday we'll say we knew you when?"

"Listen, you guys, I'll sell you my autograph right now and you can make a profit on it in ten years. Is that a deal?"

"I don't know, Josh. Ten years is a long time."

Ten years. If I lived up to my mother's and Mr. Sabbatini's expectations, in ten years I'd be . . . I didn't care. I really didn't care if I got famous and foremost like Renata Corsaro, the one who played the piano before we had it, which we didn't have yet. If I could just play the piano because I liked doing it, and nobody pressured me about fame and fortune, I'd settle for that just fine.

"Josh," someone about eight kids down the table to the right of me yelled, "are you going to be able to go out for the team this year?"

Joshua leaned forward and looked over to him, which meant he was practically in front of my face. My first impression was that by any standards this was a good-looking boy. His hair was straight and dark, and right away your eye couldn't help shifting down to his eyebrows. Most kids don't seem to have any that are noticeable—they're just part of faces and unimportant. But his were really outlined and thick. I mean, I think it gave character to his face. His eyes were a nice chocolaty shade and when he talked to his friends he kept looking straight at them until the conversation was over—like he was giving them attention without his mind wandering while the other person talked. That might not seem part of what makes a person good-looking, but the way it came at me, I couldn't help thinking of him like that. But what came into my mind next had nothing to do with his looks.

"No. I've got two Saturday matinee performances in November, so that kind of blew it for this year."

It was the way he said it that shook me up. He said it like he took it in stride. Well, I suppose he cares more about his career, whatever it is—some kind of an actor, I guess—than he does about sports or other things. He must, he sounded so sure and satisfied about his future as a celebrity. Maybe it's different with boys. They probably don't have the same feelings that girls do. What's important to them anyway? Either baseball or football or hockey, or, in the case of this Joshua kid, only his career.

One-sided, that's what boys are. No depth to them.

Still, I thought I'd stick around awhile. I looked in my lunch bag to see what other goodies my mother had put in there. An apple and a cookie. The cookie was a hermit left over from a batch of Sam's and the apple, no doubt a new-crop McIntosh. I sank my teeth into the sweet juice and pulled out a sizable bite. It *was* good.

"Eddie," Joshua called to his friend, "don't forget, today is Debating Society meeting."

"Yuh, but first we have to go to the library to find some stuff on immigration laws for the paper we're working on."

"Right. I forgot. OK, wait for me at the bike rack."

I had about two or three more chews to finish the bite of apple when that last bit of dialogue stopped me as if my jaws got paralyzed. One-sided boy? Interested only in his career? He sounded more like hundred-sided. Talented, interested in schoolwork, outside activities, and has lots of friends. What kind of monster was this? Worse, what kind of slob was I that I was having such trouble handling my present life? A far cry from my own girl, let alone my own woman.

What did Joshua have that I needed—and how do I get it?

If I was a spy, a detective-type, I guess I would have followed him around to see how he behaved, what he did and said and in general try to find out what made him tick. But I'm not that type. My mother's type, she would have buttonholed him, is what she would have done, and said something like, "Look here, young man, tell me what it is with you. Let's have the whole story." Sam would have—but I can't count him because he's male and there's a difference between the way a male and a female would tackle a situation like that. But the way Sam would find out what he wanted to would be to study his victim, unobtrusively. My type, I'd keep lowering my eyes over mushy sandwiches, swallow hard, and suffer.

Well, why not, the question pestered me. So I'll do it the way Sam would. I had to figure this kid out. I had to know. Of course there was only one small snag. How? I mean it isn't as if he were in my class or the seventh grade even. Or lived around me. I'd never seen him before, which meant he was in another elementary school district. In fact, at this time I didn't even know his last name, so it would be harder to track him down.

My Aunt Alice is a fatalist. She always says, "If it's going to happen it will happen, no matter what you do about it." She lives in Detroit so we don't get to see her much, since we live in Boston, but after what happened in school the next day, I felt like calling her long distance and telling her, "You're right, Auntie."

That was because, boom, just like that, fate put me in the same place at the same time with Joshua.

It all began when we had a seventh-grade assembly the period after everyone's lunch. The principal, Mrs. Larkin, was giving us the annual welcome speech and announcing all the marvelous opportunities for enrichment. I thought to myself, how many times do they have to stab me? I saw the list, I heard the comments. Enough already. But no —she called on all the teachers who lead the special activities program. Mr. Woods from the social studies department led off with a summary of what goes on in his challenging group entitled Civilizations in a Troubled World. It sounded more like a threat than a pleasure and I didn't think he'd get many members from the kids I knew. Mrs. Keller from home economics got rapturous about her Epicurean Club where "you learn to create delicacies of the table, gastronomical delights." It sounded like an ad for a fancy restaurant and I wondered if she was as good as Sam. There were a few more, but I was pretty successful at not paying attention. Then Mr. Foster changed everything for me.

No one knew what his club was all about until he said three or four sentences, but that was his technique for getting everyone interested. I knew right away and that's what made me forget the whole world except what he was saying. He started off with, "Have you ever listened to someone talking to you without words?" I literally moved to the edge of my seat and felt like I was smiling all over me. He was talking about a composer who talks to you through music. Then he said, "Do you know what has shape and form but can't be held in your hand?" Did I know? Boy, did I know. The next thing he threw out was, "How about this for an idea? Six people telling you the same statement, but because it is spoken at different rates of speed, you get a different message from each one." I thought I'd jump out of my skin at that like a skier when he takes off from the top of a hill and soars in the air.

What he was talking about that time was how you can take any four notes, *any,* and according to the way you play it, it can sound happy or sad or strong or weak—or anything. I tell you there was no question. I nibbled at his bait and I knew I had to go to Audition for Orchestra, Tuesday—2:30. I couldn't not have gone if my mother herself was standing at the door saying, "Gina, go home."

So the next Tuesday I tried out. But I had to explain to Lucy and Remi how come I was doing this after my big noise about the four hours daily, and how I practically had to take a plane home from school so I wouldn't miss one precious second.

"Gina," Remi said when she and Lucy were going to sign up for their clubs, "Karen isn't signing up today. She has a dentist appointment, so you'll have her to walk home with."

Never in Remi's or Lucy's wildest dreams would they have imagined that I'd be staying to join something. It was pretty embarrassing for me, but I had to tell them I wasn't going right home, with or without Karen.

"I'm—I'm going out for the school orchestra," the words popped out of my mouth.

"You're NOT!"

"What about your MOTHER!"

"I haven't told her and I might not make the orchestra anyway."

"You'll make it all right," Lucy was optimistic as usual.

"Then I'll worry about my mother later."

Remi wanted to know, "What about Mr. Sabbatini and the four-hour practice sessions?"

What could I say? That "music is everything in the world to me and I am driven to do this," which was true, or tone it down to, "Oh, I thought it would be a fun thing to do on Tuesdays," which was also true. So I did what I usually do when I'm stuck for an answer. I didn't say anything. I shrugged.

"Well, I wish you luck, Gina. With your mother *and* Mr. Sabbatini."

"Thanks, I'll need it."

I went into the auditorium where the auditions were being held and forgot about my problem. About thirty-five kids came and Mr. Foster called out to us, "Piano, over here; strings, there; woodwinds, there; and brass, here. Any percussions?" A couple of drummers yelled yes, and he told them where to wait.

Most of the auditioners were piano, which is the usual thing. I didn't notice anyone else especially, until Mr. Foster had each of us give our name and homeroom number when it was our turn. He listened to everyone separately and at the end said, "Thank you, I'll let you know."

Some of them left as soon as they were through, but after my turn, I stayed. I don't know why. Maybe I just enjoyed being in the room with all those instruments. Anyway, when Mr. Foster got to the clarinets, there was Joshua. He walked up front, said, "Joshua Jackson, Room four twelve." That was when I thought of my Aunt Alice.

Joshua did his number and he sounded pretty good. I figured he was in some kind of youth orchestra that performed out of town and that was what all those rehearsals were about. There couldn't be any important professional youth symphony or Mr. Sabbatini would have told me, so I still wasn't sure what group Joshua was connected with.

After he got through, he walked up the aisle and I watched him until he was out of sight on the other side of the door. I didn't get any clues from that whole scene and all I could do was hope we'd both make the grade so I could continue my observations.

If I had prayed I would have said my prayers were answered Thursday when I saw my name on the board to report for orchestra rehearsal the following Tuesday. I hadn't prayed at all because mainly I had other things on my mind. Such as trying to act casual when my mother talked to me about any subject at all. Suppressing information can give you an unnatural feeling and you're sure at the slightest pause that you're giving yourself away.

Then I had my lesson with Mr. Sabbatini. I was afraid he'd know by the sound that I'd missed almost one whole day because the Tuesday of tryouts I didn't get home until four o'clock.

"Bene, bene," he said after my first etude. That's praise in Italian, but it made me feel worse. I wasn't sure if he could see through me or read the sign I was sure was written all over me—Gina Barlow Cheated on Her Practicing!

The first orchestra rehearsal was the next day. That meant another day of nonpractice. How long was I going to carry this burden of deception? More to the point, how long could I carry it? I didn't even tell Sam because he and Charlie had gone out of town to do some research on country inns and wouldn't be back for another week.

"I told you you'd get picked," Lucy couldn't have been prouder if she had done it herself.

"How are you going to handle your situation at home?" Remi asked.

"Stall for now," I said.

When I came in for rehearsal after school on Tuesday and saw Joshua, my unprayed prayers came through again. Now I would go out and buy a notebook and list Observations and Conclusions and discover the solution. When I saw him laughing and fooling around with a couple of boys in the woodwind section, I was afraid I'd need a year of shadowing to figure him out. How could he take on another activity on top of all that I already knew about and be so shirt-sleeve easy? That's what he was—loose. And the longer I couldn't work out my crucial state of affairs the tighter I was getting.

"Ladies and gentlemen," Mr. Foster quieted everyone down, "as I call your names, please take your instruments to the area we shall refer to as the orchestra pit and I will assign your positions there." Then he looked at me and said, "We're going to allow you to use the school piano—unless, of course, you want to bring your own." Everyone laughed including me, which kind of tells what a nice manner he has. Even though he is nothing like Sam, he reminded me of him.

Mr. Foster told us we were going to have a Thanksgiving assembly program and we'd need two rehearsals a week for forty minutes each until the concert. A thumping started in my head that could have been the entire percussion section doing a private rehearsal of their own.

Twice a week for forty minutes each time would mean roughly eight weeks until Thanksgiving. That would be sixteen rehearsals equivalent to sixteen hours, give or take five to ten minutes. Sixteen hours subtracted from home practice time—fatal! My mother would disown me and my piano teacher would publicly flog me. My mother would make me pay her back the four thousand dollars and Mr. Sabbatini would give up his career, considering himself a failure, and it would be on my conscience the rest of my life.

On the other hand, that would give me sixteen hours, give or take a few minutes, during which I could examine the conduct of one Joshua Jackson to determine the workings of his mind so I could apply it to myself and become a new, mature, well-disciplined, un-tense, all-American girl.

Some of the kids knew each other from before and the rest of us were talking back and forth as if we had. When I say the rest of us it didn't mean every single member. Joshua and I didn't exchange one syllable. The piano is separated from the woodwinds by at least four instruments. So that took care of rehearsal number one.

Getting home later than usual was no real problem so far as my mother's finding out was concerned. She didn't get in from the spa until after five and if I had to light the oven or something like that, I had plenty of time to do it. My feeling of guilt was the problem. But I still didn't tell her.

That week passed quietly enough. We got a card from Sam who said they were going to stay a few more days to cover Vermont before heading back.

"He could give *them* lessons, he doesn't have to pick up any tips from anybody," my mother said.

It didn't surprise me at all. I knew she was proud of him. It just hurt her that he didn't live with us. Besides the father-figure business, I think she had the idea that old retired parents are supposed to live with their children.

The next week rehearsals were called for Tuesday and Thursday. At least it didn't conflict with my lesson, which was Monday. On Thursday Joshua and I finally made contact. I had been watching him as best I could and his general cheerfulness and popularity were getting on my nerves.

On my way home the Tuesday before, I had actually gone in to the variety store in the shopping center and bought a five- by eight-inch notebook that, to date, was blank. I was not about to write any headings in it such as Understanding the Behavior Patterns of Joshua Jackson. That's all my mother would need. She'd turn into the most probing psychiatrist in the country.

Thursday we were just leaving the auditorium after rehearsing one of the selections for the assembly that I had a part in. It was Burt Bacha-rach's "Close to You" and I was doing the solo introduction. Mr. Foster had said some complimentary things about the whole orchestra and me in particular and naturally I beamed like a spotlight. I was almost at the door when a voice to my left said, "You play very well, Gina." I remembered the voice before I saw the body that went with it. It came at me from the same angle as it did when I was in the lunchroom at the eighth-grade table. For no reason that I know, I felt myself getting warm from the neck up, which was not the way I reacted to Mr. Foster's compliment. I turned to Joshua on my left and said, "Thanks."

I don't think I really looked him full in the face, but I was sure that mine was in living color. Talk about behavior patterns! I didn't even understand my own. What was I so self-conscious about? That I was planning a confidential file on him?

"You've either been taking lessons for a long time or you're a natural," he smiled at me.

"Oh, I'm just a natural," I tossed it off lightly with a surprised feeling that the remark was coming from me.

He grinned as if he appreciated my humor. "Hey, that's a coincidence, so am I."

I relaxed right away and grinned back at him. It didn't even cross my mind that my braces showed.

"How do you like Brookside?" he said, obviously spotting me as a seventh grader. I thought it was pretty sharp of him. I mean, after all, it's not what you'd call a small school.

"Not bad," I said as if I were an old hand at rating junior highs.

"They've got a great foreign language department here. What are you taking?"

"Spanish."

"Me too. Do you like it?"

"Getting to. Do you?"

"*Mucho.*"

"Does it get harder the second year?"

"I guess so, but I like languages."

There he was, being positive. I wondered if there was anything he *didn't* like.

"Gina, we're over here." It was Remi calling from near the front door where she was waiting for me with Lucy. They had stayed for their groups on Creative Movement and Greenhouses. The last time the three of us had gone over possible careers, Remi was considering dancing and Lucy had her heart set on plant pathology, which accounted for their choices in after-school clubs.

"OK," I called to them and turned to Joshua. "See you Tuesday," I said.

"If not before," he sort of nodded me good-bye.

I stood there for a couple of seconds looking at him as he walked down the hall. I was thinking nothing in particular—maybe just an awareness that he was a nice kid. Somehow, he didn't get my nerves on edge at all. Then I walked over to the girls.

"Who was that cute boy, Gina?" Lucy was at the drooling point.

"He's a-*dora*ble," Remi agreed.

Was he? I was just about to tell them that his looks had escaped me when they began asking more questions about him. And instead of giving them an honest and complete rundown on Joshua Jackson from the beginning, all I was telling them was that he was one of the clarinetists from the orchestra.

It occurred to me that I was now harboring two secrets: one from my mother and piano teacher and the other from my friends. Was this the kind of thing that happens to everyone when they get older?

That night when I went up to my room, I took out the notebook. I gazed at the blank pages and then went to bed leaving them as they were before.

7 From then on Joshua and I spoke to each other on an average of three times a day. It's funny—if you don't know someone you can pass him in the hall a hundred times and not know he's there. But once you know him, you keep seeing him all over the place.

Every time we met it seemed we managed to get in a couple of lines of dialogue. They weren't always sparkling with wit, but that wasn't necessary. We only had to wave and say "hi" and it gave me a better feeling than I had the moment before. And then, somehow, our conversations got to be more important—not just "hi" or trying to show each other how clever we were with smart cracks. Oh, we didn't talk about the problems of the world or anything like that. Actually it wasn't the subject matter that made the change. I think it was that we were getting to be friends.

Like the Monday Joshua found out he couldn't come to orchestra rehearsal the next day because there was a conflict with the choral group he had joined. Actually it was the school's mistake in scheduling, which they corrected by the next week, but when it happened, I was the one who Joshua told first.

"Gina, I'd much rather go to orchestra, but choral has priority."

"How come?"

"On account of my singing."

"What, on account of your singing?"

He looked at me first in surprise and then his eyebrows got back in place. "Oh, I guess you didn't know. I sing with the Met."

"The Met?"

"Yuh, you know, the Metropolitan—the opera." He said it so simply he could have been saying, "I saw a good show on TV last night."

"The Metropolitan Opera!" I fairly shrieked it at him and if prizes were given out for The Most Surprised Expression, I would have won. "Why didn't you tell me?"

"Oh, I dunno." He seemed almost indifferent, but I know it was only modesty.

"Oh, my gosh!" Those were the rehearsals he'd been talking about with his friend Eddie. "That explains it. Oh, wow!"

"What does it explain?"

"Never mind, just tell me *everything!* How do you have the *time?*" I shrieked at him again.

"No problem with time if the dumb school gets their schedules straight." He sounded miffed again about missing orchestra rehearsal.

I was having trouble sorting out all the questions that had tumbled into my brain. Questions I'd had before plus some new ones. For instance, how come his family let him do all those extracurricular things if he was a professional already? And how could he be so relaxed and how did he get *in* to the Met in the first place? So I just put it all to him point-blank.

He listened and thought about the first two parts, staring into space and frowning. "I don't know, that's the way it is, I guess." For the third part he was more relaxed again and had some facts.

"My uncle Ron lives in New York and the boss of his company is related to an executive in the Met."

"Oh, connections," I said knowingly.

"Only for the introduction," he assured me. "But I had to try out at their regular auditions two years ago and I made the children's chorus. This year I'm going to sing my first solo." He face looked as if he were standing next to a rainbow. "I'm going to sing Fyodor, the son of the czar in *Boris Godunov*."

I could tell what he must be feeling inside him. Something like I felt when Mr. Foster spoke to the seventh-grade assembly or when I practice and feel that me and the music are two parts together that make one whole. And it didn't matter that I hadn't got a satisfactory answer to my other questions. There we were, standing outside my science class and it was time for the period to start and all the kids had already gone in. Looking at Joshua with the glow in his eyes and me understanding it, it didn't make any difference what time it was or that I'd be late for my favorite subject.

A couple of other things slipped into my mind. I remembered that the notebook I'd bought was still empty. What struck me most was that I had completely forgotten about writing in it. And the other thing was that I'd never told Joshua about my practicing conflicting with anything else I wanted to do or that my mother didn't know I was in the orchestra. It wasn't that I'd deliberately held back, but the occasion to say those things hadn't come up. At that minute I was dying to tell him. I'd have given anything to get it off my chest, right then—to him. But something kept me from it and I knew clearly what it was. I couldn't say one thing that would spoil that terrific sensation he was having thinking about his solo performance. I hadn't even said how great I thought that was, but it wouldn't have made any difference . . . he might not even have heard any words from the outside. So I just lightly touched his sleeve and said, "We'd better go. We'll be late."

He came back to the present and said, "Yuh, I'll have to tell Mr. Foster today."

I was in a strange, almost dazed state all through science, which is unusual, and all through math, which is more or less usual. After school, when we were walking home, Lucy wanted to know how long I was going to keep it from my mother, about the orchestra.

"Gina, postponing it isn't going to make it any easier when the time comes, you know."

"I know."

"While we're on the subject of keeping things from people, I think you're keeping something from us," Remi said accusingly.

I was afraid I knew what she meant. I hadn't told them that Joshua wasn't "just one of the clarinetists in the orchestra." They knew me well enough to spot that I wasn't letting on about something.

"I think," Remi went on without waiting for me to defend myself, "that you have a boyfriend and you're not telling us."

I know I got red. The kids had been giving me details since the second day at Brookside about the eye and hair color of at least sixty-seven boys in the school. If a boy so much as said one word to Remi, I heard about it a million times. Their being free with their information made it worse for me because if someone holds back on you, you don't mind so much if you're not one hundred percent honest with them. But that day was not the time for me to tell anybody anything. I wanted to be left alone so I could work out some things in my mind.

I gave them what I'm sure was a sick smile and said, "Why wouldn't I tell you if I had a boyfriend?"

"That's a good question," Remi said.

"Well, the answer is I don't have a boyfriend." Joshua was not my boyfriend in the sense that they meant it, I rationalized. He was a regular friend.

Lucy came to my rescue. "OK, if you *get* a boyfriend, promise to tell us immediately?"

"I promise."

So we parted on good terms and about a half a block from home I came to a very definite, very determined decision. This time for sure I was going to announce to my mother that no longer was I going to deprive myself of anything. I'm going to eat my cake and I'm going to have it too. The world is my oyster, Mom, I was going to say to her. I wasn't quite sure what that meant except it's something good. Joshua himself said he has time for everything and that's the way it's going to be with me!

I increased my speed almost to a run and got to my house and bounced up the front steps. I knew Mom would be home when I got there because she hadn't gone to the spa that day. Due to conditions beyond her control, to quote her, she caught a virus from one of her clients. "If I've told them once I've told them a thousand times—'If you feel a cold coming on, nurse it on your own home grounds, not here where you can infect an entire community.' But do they pay attention? No!" And then she had sneezed and crawled under the covers.

I swung open the door as if it were set to a rhythmic beat and I took a big breath. I would say, "Hello, Mom, how are you?" and then spring upstairs to her bedroom and let it all out.

"Sam, I don't care if you *are* my father. Gina is my daughter and I'll make the decisions!"

Mom was yelling from upstairs and Sam was

there. I hadn't noticed his car in the driveway I'd been so excited to get in the house.

"I'd say, Evelyn, that a few of those decisions haven't been too smart."

"That's your opinion. For me, I think they've been smart. But even if they weren't, they were my decisions to make. You aren't on the scene anymore. By your own choosing, I might add."

There was a silence and I knew they were giving each other the stares. My head was whirring. Sam must have made a special trip here to tell Mom face-to-face how upset I was. Only, if I knew Sam, he wouldn't let her know I'd made any complaints.

"Evvy, you're wrong." Sam's voice was so quiet, it was like when I'm playing Debussy's first nocturne, "Clouds." Peaceful and serene. What Mr. Sabbatini calls *pacevelo* and *sireno*. But what was going on upstairs was an argument, which usually means yelling and screaming by both parties.

"You're making a big mistake," Sam was controlling his anger, "to put yourself in debt to the piano company to the tune, if I may make a pun, to the tune of four thousand dollars."

I remembered our telephone conversation. He had said we had to be subtle. What he just said didn't sound subtle to me.

"Sam, Gina is an artist and an artist requires the best tools."

I wished Mom wouldn't talk like that, making me feel I had so much to live up to. Oh, Sam, say the right thing to her.

"I know she has talent," he said gently and left a gap between that and the rest of his sentence.

Sam, that's too subtle—she won't catch on!

And then he finished, leaving out any possible hidden meanings. "But a four-thousand-dollar instrument puts too much of a burden on a child."

Mom said her say with passion. "Not to keep faith with your talent is a sin!"

She couldn't have done it better if she'd been on stage. The only problem was, she meant it, she wasn't acting, which just put my planned speech behind the eight ball for good.

My second try at telling my mother about my oyster went *pfftt*. Now what? It lay there like a bundle of unrecycled trash marked for City Dump.

"And, Sam," Mom's voice cracked and I didn't know if it was from her virus or her emotion, "don't you realize that a woman *has* to have a career these days?"

I thought sure she'd get laryngitis when the end of that sentence came, she had strained her voice so much to get there.

After that there was a big blank as if you were watching TV and the screen suddenly went white and soundless. I could feel pain in my grandfather's silence. He never thought people should have to do anything they didn't really believe in, regardless of public opinion. But Sam doesn't make a big noisy fight like a lot of people do to push their points across. He only said, "How about letting Gina make her own choice, Evvy?"

Bless you, Sam. But I had my doubts about any effect his understanding would have on my mother. And if it did get across to her, I hoped she wouldn't think that meant I wanted to give up the piano entirely. If push ever came to shove, like Sam says once in a while, I—I honestly don't know which way I'd go.

There was another silence and Sam stopped it with a remark that scared me. "Has it occurred to you that you're living Gina's life for her instead of living your own, Evvy?"

I got close to panic hearing that. That was going to be like opening a can of worms. Mom would be furious about his accusation and then he'd tell her again she ought to get married and she'd object and he'd look at her with his I-know-you-so-well-look and . . . I'd be in the middle of the whole mess.

Mom started a coughing seizure and I don't know for sure if it was real on account of her cold or real on account of her indignation. But that was the end of it and I knew Sam was about ready to leave. I had to make up my mind fast whether I would go out and come back in as if for the first time, or run over to the piano and start the Moonlight Sonata. I figured I'd better do the first one—there'd be no questions to answer. So that's what I did.

I stood in front of the door deciding whether I'd ring the bell to let them know I'd just arrived and hadn't heard a thing, or use my key, barge in, and yell, "Hi, Mom, I'm home, how are you?" the way I'd planned before. I thought, maybe if I'd been born in an earlier century, I'd have made it big. No decisions about a career—just marry and have kids. They had it easy in those days.

8 I was slouching at my desk in math while Mr. Powers was writing some complicated X equations on the board. That was my life—the biggest complicated X anyone could fit on any chalk board in the school. In the world, in fact.

No, I'm not a complicated X. I am a very simple slob. I'm an emotional and intellectual slob. I am an emotional and an intellectual slob and a character weakling.

I let those descriptions of me run around in my head seven or eight times for emphasis until a low groan coming out of my own throat brought me to a sudden sit-up position. I looked down at the white paper on my desk that I was supposed to cover with those equations plus their solutions. Well, OK, next period I'd go back to self-recrimination during Europeans Exploring the American Continent. I couldn't afford too much attention-wandering in math.

Next period the Europeans did about fifty years of exploration before my mind got back to myself, personally. It was when I was walking down the hall on my way to art that I realized I hadn't seen Joshua once that day. I kept looking at everyone who passed and no one was Joshua. By the time I was beside the door of the art class I didn't want to go in. I gave the hall, as far as I could see, another long look. It was already empty of people, but I stared for a few seconds more and then I got the funniest lonely feeling.

I'd felt lonely before, plenty of times, but it was a different feeling than this. Yesterday afternoon when I'd gone back outside the front door, I'd had a lonely feeling. But when Sam opened the door before I got to it, I clean forgot about feeling lost and hugged him with all my strength. Sam gave it right back to me too. We didn't make up fakes about, "Oh, I didn't know you were here" or "I was in the neighborhood and thought I'd drop in." None of that stuff. After we separated from the hugs, I looked up at him and smiled and he looked down at me and sent out comforting messages with his eyes. He meant it to be comforting, but even if I hadn't heard what had gone on upstairs, I'd have known from his face that my problem was still unsolved. His out-loud words said, "It's going to work out, Gina. I'll be in touch very soon." Then when he started down the steps he turned and said, "Don't get your mother's cold."

I heard myself say, "Sure, OK, Grandpa." It sort of slipped out. I never say "Grandpa."

When I'd gone up to Mom's bedroom to ask her if she needed anything after Sam left, I was reciting silently, with a thousand bolts of fright charging through my body, what I'd planned.

"There's this boy, Mom. He has about twelve different activities including his professional career that he commutes to New York for. He loves his singing the same as I love the piano and his parents encourage him to do anything he wants in addition. *Encourage* him, Mom!"

But that little speech didn't get any further than the inside of my head. Mom had her own speech waiting for me when I got there. Not about Sam. She acted as if he had never set foot in the house and, contrary to what she told her clients to do in case of sickness, she informed me she was going to the spa the next day even if she was still contagious. She would keep to herself in her office and go over her accounts and read up on some new therapy methods. I could use a few myself, but I didn't say that. At least I was free to go to orchestra and not worry that she'd ask me where I was after school.

I was lonely that night too, no matter how much I thought of Sam. But that was a different kind of loneliness again. That one was because I wished my mother was more like Sam. Whatever part of her was the same, it didn't show when I wanted it to. Enough of the time, anyway.

So here I was, standing at the doorway of Room 314, with a brand-new type of lonely feeling. If Joshua were only here. Right now. I'd tell him everything. I'd say, "Boy, Joshua, if you knew the cowardly person I really am, you wouldn't have one thing to do with me." And then he'd say, "You are not a cowardly person, Gina. You are a girl of great courage." And then I'd say, "But, Joshua, I am an ingrate, a sneak and I cause arguments between those I love." Then he'd put his hand up to quiet my despair and he would say, "Not another word. I will not hear you utter slander against yourself or defame your perfect character." That's what Joshua would say.

"Hey, Gina, wait 'til you see what we're going to do today in art!" Jody clutched my arm, and my wishful-thinking bubble burst.

I took a good, deep breath and went in to find out what fantastic thing we were going to do in art. It wasn't much, really.

Always during orchestra rehearsal I am aware in my mind that even though I can't see him over in the woodwind section, I know Joshua is sitting there. I mean it's no revolutionary deal. I just know he's there and that's that. The day he wasn't there was one big upheaval of a deal. If it was try-out time for piano players, I would never have made it. Wrong notes, nothing. My timing was off, and my phrasing—I couldn't even make "Tea for Two" sound good.

Mr. Foster was nice about it though. Not once did he call attention to my mistakes. Verbally, that is. He looked at me a couple of times, frowning and obviously wondering what was going on, while I snapped my head down as if my life depended on getting some kind of clue from the keyboard, which I didn't get.

For some crazy mixed-up reason, who knows why, instead of going home after orchestra, I walked to the spa. I hadn't done that for years, so I don't know what possessed me then—particularly since if I used my head I'd have known I'd get questioned about what happened to my daily schedule, which my mother thought I was following. So it was quite a risk I was taking, but I didn't give it a thought. I guess my mind was more a blank than a container for thoughts all the time it took me to get there.

The Evelyn Barlow Physical Fitness Spa is a much better reflection of my mother's personality than our house is. It's like Mom's other self took over the furnishing when she went out in the real world and got into business. Even starting from the enormous black and brass double front doors with giant brass loopy handles, on into the reception area with gold and white shimmering tile floors, and all through the whole building with the saunas and pools and a place called the Eucalyptus Inhalation Room, it's modern up to the roots of her hair. I've noticed lately though, a few gray hairs at her roots, which Mom says are premature, but she also says she has no intention of making any color alterations. "I accept and am grateful for what nature gives me—the same as I am about the talent nature has given you, Gina."

I cringed when she said that. It was the first day of junior high—the day that Mom discovered the gray in her hair and I discovered a world bigger than Bach, Beethoven, and Brahms.

Ted Richards was standing on the other side of the huge doors with his manufactured smile to welcome what he hoped was a client. I don't know what his official title is, but if Ted were a girl you'd call him a hostess. He gives everyone the big hello, oozes what he thinks is warmth and friendliness, and tries to get them to join the club. It's a mystery to me how my mother can stand having him around. He must have a contract that came with the building and equipment.

"Hello, Gina. Where have you been *keeping* yourself? We haven't seen you in a month of Sundays."

He makes me nauseous.

"Oh, school, you know." I tried to look pleasant.

"Bet you've got a boyfriend already." He thought he was absolutely *devilish* as he raised both eyebrows and worked his smile.

Fortunately I didn't blush. Mostly because I wasn't embarrassed. Just sickened.

"Not really," I said.

"Shall I buzz your mom to let her know you're

here?" His eyebrows were still up around his skull.

"No, thank you. That won't be necessary," I told him, walking toward the hall that leads to her office. "See you." I managed a smile.

"Don't be such a stranger, Gina. Come see us more often," he sang that at me, referring to himself as "us." I don't understand what kind of an act that is when people talk like that. I mean everybody's been to school! *Us* is plural. *Me* is singular.

Mom was at her desk with the telephone about six inches away from her ear, so she could look into the mouthpiece as if the one she was talking to were there in person.

"No! Really? You *mean* it?"

Then she leaned her head back and looked up to the ceiling with an expression like Mr. Sabbatini when it seemed he was getting spiritual messages from the plaster. "Gracie, that is something to *think* about."

Gracie is Mom's best friend from their diaper days. It's a funny thing but, even though my mom comes through as a dynamo in making her own decisions like the way she told Sam the day before, she sure gets a lot of input from Gracie. Not on big things like whether she should go into business —it's more like information. She's the one who told Mom that there was such a thing in the world as a partly used grand piano for half the price of a new one. Mom is usually so involved with what she's doing that she doesn't take the time to get in on outside happenings. Gracie acts as a one-woman information center for her entire circle of friends. If someone wants to know what's a good movie, which store is having a sale, or who got married, got divorced, or died, the fastest way to find out is to ask Gracie. And you feel you've hit the jackpot when you don't get a busy signal on her phone. I don't know who called who that afternoon, but I could tell that Mom was enjoying some new bits of knowledge. Maybe a half-priced vitamin outlet opened in the neighborhood.

I stood there waiting until she finished without clearing my throat to make her aware of my presence. She happened to look up and interrupted Gracie. "I'll call you back later. Gina just came in."

She turned to me in astonishment and said, "Gina, what's the matter? Did you eat? Did you practice? What are you doing here? Is something wrong?"

I noticed that Mom's priority on food had the edge over my practicing. You'd have thought that would have made it easier for me to tell her what I'd planned for the last two or three weeks, but I didn't even open my mouth. Boy, if we can send people to the moon, why couldn't there be an electronic gadget on me, to relieve me of the responsibility of confessing, that would light up and blare: Evelyn, your daughter has a split personality—she is part serious concert artist, part playgirl!!!!!

But no lights, no statements, and I stood mute.

"Gina," Mom stood up and repeated her questions.

"I'm OK, Mom. No, I guess I didn't eat. I—I just felt like coming here. How are you feeling?" I asked as an afterthought.

"I'm fine, fine. Come into the kitchen. You can at least have some carrot juice and wheat crackers."

That's what my mother allows her overweight members for a snack after a workout. I accepted because I suddenly realized I was hungry enough to make even that taste good.

Mom had her arm around me as we walked down the stairs to the refrigerator. Only because of the news she had just received from Gracie did she fail to demand an answer to her musical question. I wasn't looking at her face since we were walking, but from the tone of her next remarks, I knew what exalted happiness it must have shown.

"Gina, that was Gracie on the phone."

Well I knew that.

"She just gave me the most exciting piece of information you could imagine!"

I could imagine.

"There is a school in New York," Mom was speaking slowly and deliberately and I was getting less sure about what Gracie's news was. "A school that teaches all the regular subjects *plus*, it is especially for children talented in music!"

Mom stopped walking, took her arm off my shoulders, and faced me while she waited for my reaction.

"So?" I sounded husky. She couldn't mean what I was afraid she was thinking.

"So—o—I am going to make inquiries about an application and . . ."

"Mom, you aren't!"

"Gina, it's the opportunity of a lifetime. Besides the training you'll get, it's as good as a—an employment agency. That's where talent scouts look for soloists. That's where careers are made. I'm just turning over in my mind whether to sell the spa or open a branch in New York."

9 I'll practice eight hours a day, not four. If it will be any help, I'll manage so I can run over to the spa and serve carrot juice at snacktime. I'll personally try to slim those forty-five-year-old fats down to Royal Ballet size. I'll get Ted Richards a black and gold uniform. I'll do anything! But I will not go to New York. I will not leave Brookside.

All at once I knew that Brookside Junior High School with the monster-sized eighth- and ninth-grade persons of both sexes, the noisy confusion, and the general mishmash was the loveliest, the most precious thing in my life. I could not leave it. I would not leave my friends, I would not leave my orchestra, and I would not leave—Joshua! All this I knew before we got to the kitchen where the carrot juice my mother poured for me tasted like vinegar.

I think the reason I didn't say any of that to my mother was because my tongue was in a state of deep freeze. It simply wouldn't function. My stomach was churning and when I think of even the meaning of the word, I can get bilious. *To churn* is to agitate cream; *agitate,* meaning shaking until the cream is solidified. *Yicch!* My heart was also activated to a rapid pace—adagio or maybe even presto allegro. If it was being recorded on an electrocardiogram machine, it would have registered hyperkinetic. But my tongue . . . numb.

Mom sure must have thought she convinced or inspired me because by the time I left her to go home and turn on the warming oven for the pot roast, all I did was act as if I'd lost the power of speech. Which happened to be right, but when you get down to it, I didn't give her any reason to think I felt any real opposition to her plan.

Almost every step I took on the way home I kept asking myself, Why? A whole list of *why*'s. Why number one: Why does my mother have to get such wild ideas? A four-thousand-dollar piano, selling her business, which she nearly broke her neck trying to build up, and now she thinks about leaving the city of her birth. No loyalty. If people kept doing that all over the country, nobody would have any feeling of roots or any basis for remembering the good old days with the same group of childhood friends or scads of important things.

Why number two: Why'd I have to have this talent? I think it was all a lie anyway. Mr. Sabbatini made it up so he could hang on to his pupil. He probably told that to every parent whose kid was a pupil of his. He sold the idea to my mother and I was getting the idea to sue him for misrepresentation and advantage-taking of an innocent widow.

Why number three was the one that hurt the most. Why don't I stand up to my mother and tell her the truth about my life. A life that was being nipped in the bud and I'd never be able to realize its fulfillment. My enrichment unenriched before it got over the poverty level.

I guess I was at my lowest ebb at the moment I unlocked the front door and heard the phone ring. I won't answer it. I mean, who could it be to make it worth my while to pick up the receiver?

It could be one of my mother's friends, prob ably Gracie, with more smashing information to turn my life upside down. Or it could be one of my own friends, but considering my dark present state and future prospects, it would mean a separate conversation of explanations and I couldn't bring myself to go through that. It could even be Sam on the other side of that telephone line and I still couldn't face it. I walked right through the front hall and challenged, "Ring all night, I'm ignoring you."

You'd think the phone was human and obeying me. The rings got so insistent I would have sworn they were getting louder with each successive round.

"Shut up!" I commanded it as I turned the oven to three hundred degrees. I got the stuff to make the salad and I slammed the refrigerator door so hard I could hear some of the jars jiggle that were loosely stacked on the shelves. Who cares.

OK, OK, I'm COMING. I trounced into the hall and picked up the stupid receiver. "Hello," I barked.

"Gina, this is Joshua. I've been trying you for an hour. Where have you been?"

I blinked at the head of lettuce in my right hand while my left hand almost let go of the phone. This had to be fate, I told myself. This time I would definitely call Aunt Alice in Detroit.

"Auntie," I would tell her, "I'd been needing to talk to a friend of mine about a problem I've had . . . never mind the problem," I'd say as she'd ask me what it was in a worried voice. "The problem has disappeared—evaporated, since I've talked to him about it. But the point, Auntie, the point is that if it had been up to me, I'd never have been able to bring it up. But here's this great friend of mine, Joshua Jackson, who must have been reading my mind and is very sensitive to my feelings and he knew something was wrong and he called me to find out what it was. Auntie, that is what you've always said—if it's going to happen it will happen and the best thing is not to worry."

Going through that conversation in my mind, I could almost hardly wait to arrange a meeting with Joshua and hang up so I could call Detroit.

"Are you there, Gina?" Joshua's voice had an impatience I hadn't heard before. Maybe it was concern, that was it. He'd been so anxious about me it was coming out in the quality of his speech.

"I'm here, Joshua. I was at my mother's office and just got home." Little did he know what I'd found out in my mother's office, but now it would all come out right.

"Uh, how was rehearsal?"

That seemed like a long time ago. I thought back. "It was OK." I didn't have to go into details. "How was your choral group?"

He didn't answer right away and I thought we got disconnected. Then I heard an unmistakable sigh. What a guy, he's really taking my problem to heart. So I asked him again and made my voice practically cheerful. "You were the star performer, I'll bet," I ended with.

"When do you have lunch tomorrow?" he asked me with no connection to anything we had said so far.

"C Block," I said. Oh, beautiful C Block tomorrow. Joshua will figure out everything. With his ability to handle his own crowded schedule and his experience with agreeable parents, he'll work out things for me before I'm half through with my pot roast sandwich.

"I've got C Block lunch tomorrow, too. Will you meet me by the side entrance on the dot of eleven-thirty? I—I want to talk to you about something."

I felt relieved already. "Sure, Joshua."

Layers of heavy weights were dissolving off my back and by the time my mother came home you'd have thought I was in heaven with any proposition she would offer for the rest of the evening. Not that I said anything positive about going to New York or even brought up the question of where would they deliver the piano, but I didn't have anything negative to say about anything. So far as she knew I was with her all the way.

I practiced for a while after dinner and when Mom got a call from Harry Stephens, I went upstairs with a fairly clear head to do some homework.

"Gina, I think I'll call them long distance. Why waste time writing away for an application."

She said that as a statement, not a question, the next morning over breakfast. She was so preoccupied with the New York School of Music that she wasn't even watching my food consumption. My personal situation wasn't solved yet so my appetite wasn't all that big. But I was at least eating above the range where she nags me and she didn't even notice.

I didn't make any answer to her statement. It didn't make much difference if it took one week or one month for them to get their application back. Joshua was going to make a miracle that day at 11:30 on the dot.

Instead of the usual corner where Lucy and Remi meet me, they were halfway down my street when I got to my bottom step.

"Come on," Remi was signaling me wildly.

"It's not late," I said running to join them. "What's up?"

"I tried to get you on the phone last night but your line was busy." Remi was grinning with an expression as if some boy presented her with a gallon of Arpege.

Lucy filled in. "Gina, our friend Remi Martin is the first one of us to have a bona fide, genuine, real-live date. What do you think of that?"

"I think it's SUPER!" I was already so psyched up it seemed a very natural thing to have all kinds of spectacular events happen. Lucy would be next.

"Who? When? Where?" I asked.

"In the order of your questions," Remi was preening herself as we turned the corner, "an eighth-grade boy, if you don't mind. Gary Robinson. He's the handsomest!"

Remi grades boys' good looks on their hair shade. The lighter the color, the handsomer she thinks they are. Gary must be albino.

"He sits next to me in Current Issues and asked me to the Thanksgiving Dance!" Girl of the Year was written all over Remi's face.

"You can see how much he wants her to go. It's at least a month away." Lucy elaborated on the importance of Gary's invitation.

"I'll say," I agreed. Something clicked, noiselessly, in my brain. Maybe that's what Joshua wants to talk to me about. Well, all right! After I accepted, then he'd bring up how he noticed I was bothered about something and how this would be a good time to discuss it. Sure—two terrific things happening today at 11:30.

"Which means," Lucy was still referring to the length of time until the dance, "that you and I, Gina, have less than one month to get asked."

If Joshua hadn't called, I'd have thought Lucy's idea was an impossible dream, but for myself, of course, I had no doubts now that I'd be going. And it was likely that Lucy wouldn't get a date. Not that there was anything wrong with her, but maybe there were twice as many girls in the school as boys . . . maybe all the boys she'd want would ask someone else . . . or maybe most seventh-grade girls don't get asked at all. So since there was a pretty good chance Lucy would get left out, I said, "Girls can ask boys, can't they? I don't think we have to be inhibited."

"I will not ask any boy. I'd rather not go!"

"Would *you* invite a boy, Gina?" The way Remi emphasized the word *you,* she didn't think I would. She was right, but if Lucy didn't get asked I wanted her to know I thought it was OK for girls to do their own asking.

"Sure," I said, "we've got equal rights."

"Well, maybe," Lucy conceded hesitatingly, not completely sure.

Classes that morning dragged. Naturally. When you're waiting for something good to take place, time passes just the opposite from when you don't look forward to an event. Like two years ago spring when a date was set for me to have my tonsils out. I was in no hurry at all to go to the hospital, get anesthetized, operated on, and suffer a sore throat for a week afterward. But time whizzed by as if it had a plane to catch. It turned out it wasn't as bad as I expected, but nobody could convince me of that while I was sweating it out.

It was 11:25 in math and I started making body motions to stand up and leave the room. Those last five minutes were the longest in the history of my life to that date. I couldn't take my eyes off the clock and the minute hand moved like a three-wheeled bike pulling a ton of bricks over a freshly tarred road. Eleven-twenty-nine and a half. My heart beat out the last thirty seconds in time with the clock. Eleven-thirty. I made it to the side entrance of the lunch room in ten seconds flat.

I didn't have to pick my way through a throng of people or search for faces in a crowd. Joshua was already there. We saw each other at the same moment and again I felt a gradual dwindling of weight from my shoulders. By the time we said "hi," I didn't have a care in the world.

"Have you got your lunch with you?"

"Yes. Do you?"

He nodded. "Let's go out on the patio. It's OK to eat there as long as we throw the litter in the trash can."

"Sure," I said.

We went outside and sat on the steps that lead to the playground. Nobody was having gym and we were pretty much by ourselves. I unwrapped my sandwich and to start the conversation said, "What kind of sandwich do you have?"

"Cream cheese and olive." He took a half-hearted bite and began chewing as if he had rubber bands in his mouth.

"What's wrong?" I asked him leaning over, getting sort of under his chin.

He looked me straight-center in the eye. "Gina," I thought he was going to break down, "I've got a terrible problem and I think you're the only one who can help me."

Wow, is that the way boys ask for dates? What's he going to say when he comes to solving *my* problem? Will he have a tantrum on the floor?

"Be glad to help."

He took another bite, finished the elastic mouthful, and said, "My parents. They're giving me a hard time."

His parents didn't want him going out on dates. He was too young. Well, I'd understand. The dance wasn't that important. If nobody else asked me, I wouldn't go, that's all. What was the big deal? The beautiful relationship we had between us was the thing that mattered to me.

"That's OK, Joshua," I said with what I felt was deep, mutual rapport.

"OK that my parents are giving me a hard time? You think that's OK?"

I'd been thinking so hard analyzing what he had said, I'd answered him as if my thoughts had spoken. "Oh, I mean . . . it'll come out all right." I hoped I made a successful recovery.

"You don't know the half of it."

I was afraid to utter a syllable or blink an eyelid. I was not about to make a wrong move. This certainly seemed a funny way to get into the kind of conversation we were supposed to be having. I swallowed and hoped he didn't hear it.

"You're so cool, Gina. You've got it so all together. How do you do it?"

I was cool? How did I . . . ? What was he talking about?

"I'll bet you do as many things as I do . . . maybe more. You've got all that practicing every day, you're in the orchestra, and you even go to your mother's office and you keep so—cool. Nothing bothers you."

Was he serious? Did he think I helped my mother run her business? I scanned his face carefully. It looked like he meant what he said. No reason for him not to, I suppose. I never had got around to telling him what my life was really like.

"My mother thinks I'm going to crack up," he said earnestly.

"Joshua, what are you talking about?"

"My father says it's pretty obvious I can't handle the heavy program I'm carrying. You know what he did? He made a list on a long, skinny piece of paper, like the price sheet for a month's supply of food from the supermarket. Then he read it off as if it were some stock market report. 'Debating—Monday three; Choral Group—Monday four; Clarinet Lesson—Wednesday three-thirty; Orchestra—Tuesdays and Thursdays two-thirty; Metropolitan Opera Schedule—frequently; School Work—whenever you can squeeze it in.' " Joshua was scowling the way he must have looked at his father while he was going over the list. Then he turned to me, absolutely forlorn.

This had to be a mistake. Or a fantasy of mine. I could just hear Remi's father, Dr. Martin. "This is a subconscious fabrication, Gina, a transferral of your own problems on to someone else."

I shook my head a couple of times as if to clear the fog inside it. Yuh, there was Joshua sitting beside me with his pile of books and the wax paper from his cream cheese and olive, and his very sad expression. I looked down at my lap. I was half through with my pot roast sandwich and we hadn't got anywhere near my problem, let alone come up with a solution. He wasn't going to ask me to the dance. He wasn't going to help me out of my awful situation. HE wasn't even aware I had an awful situation. I was the one who was going to crack up.

"I thought you said your parents didn't object to all the things you're involved in."

"They didn't in the beginning. First they told me to go ahead and do whatever I wanted and then when I did they found something to object to. I can't help it if there are schedule conflicts."

"You mean the one with orchestra rehearsal and choral group?"

"For one thing." He said it angrily as if I were a stand-in for his parents.

"That's going to be changed," I said easily, eliminating that complication.

"But that's not the only thing they're making waves about."

"From the way you act, nobody'd know you were having any problems. You're so—so easygoing." I couldn't sound out the word *cool*. He'd used it on me. I had it all together, did I? Boy, if he only knew what was going on in my mind, my emotions, my whole psyche. Maybe it was just a front with him, too? I asked him.

"No," he shook his head thoughtfully. "I just happen to love doing the thing I'm doing when I'm doing it."

Me too, in a way. But he was lucky. A clarinet didn't cost like a baby-grand piano and there was no financial outlay at all for singing. You just open your mouth and there it is.

"Are your parents forcing you to—to be in the opera?" I held my breath for his answer. Maybe that was his big conflict, like me and my four hours.

"*Forcing* me?" He opened his eyes as wide as they could go and I thought he was going to burst out laughing. "That's the trouble. I can hardly wait for every performance to begin—I love it. There's nothing I want to give up. Every year there are more things I want to do. And this year . . ." He suddenly got very sober and didn't finish his sentence. He just looked at his partly eaten lunch and moved his lips to a hopeless pout.

"What happened this year?" I prodded him.

"This year, there are—well different things. A lot of stuff." He said that in a grumble and then his voice changed to how it must have been if he yelled at his father. "How can I go to the Thanksgiving Dance if I'm performing in New York on the same night?"

The fact that I recognized that I was being asked to the Thanksgiving Dance wasn't, at that moment, of any big importance. What was waking my mind up with importance was that Joshua Jackson, boy wonder, had a problem that was almost identical with mine. The only significant difference was that his parents knew exactly what he was doing with his time and what he wanted to do with the time he didn't have. And another very significant fact was that Joshua needed me to solve his problem instead of the other way around.

10 Before 11:45 I'd made a pretty big discovery. It's just as hard to work out somebody else's problems as it is to work out your own.

Right after I was aware of the sensational thing Joshua said, I felt I could cope with anything. The President of the United States could ask me, and like that, with a snap of my fingers, I could arrange a perfect world. Then I got down to solutions for Joshua. The first thing I said was, "You're going to go to a million dances in your lifetime, but if you don't show up for a performance of the Metropolitan Opera, they'll never depend on you again. And what kind of faith will you have in yourself if you do that?"

He had raised his head and turned to face me. He stayed in that position all through the rest of our conversation as if some magnet were holding him there. He didn't say anything after those opening remarks, but he was sure looking at me very intently.

"You've got an important career waiting for you and you don't get that just by waving a magic wand, you know."

Those pearls of wisdom were coming out of my mouth like snowflakes falling one after the other. If someone, for example, my English teacher, had asked me to prepare a pep talk as an assignment, I wouldn't have known where to start or what to put in it. But that C Block, sitting on the steps of the side entrance to the Brookside Junior High School lunchroom, you'd have thought I was a professional pep-talk composer. At first I didn't know where those ideas were coming from, but after about the third encouraging statement, it began to sound familiar to me. By the time I got to say, "You have to be willing to sacrifice a less important thing for a bigger thing," I knew where I'd heard it all before.

From my mother.

That was what she'd been telling me for weeks. The same information that left me cold, I was now turning over to Joshua. But the kooky thing was that I meant what I was saying and that made it sound very convincing. Finally I stopped talking and waited for his reaction.

Without moving a muscle, he said, "You're fantastic."

Boy, did that set me up. I couldn't get over my success. No time at all and I had straightened him out.

"One hundred percent fantastic," he repeated and added to it.

He didn't change the angle of his head, but his eyes had a different look. Was it admiration and awe, or surprise that I could convince him so easily?

"I should have known," he went on.

"What should you have known?" I tried to sound modest.

"I should have known better!" His voice gained volume like a crescendo. "That is exactly the kind of talk I've been getting from my parents. I certainly thought I'd hear something different from a—a friend." He was near shouting by then and I couldn't tell if the expression in his eyes was rage or scorn. "I should have known not to expect anything better . . . from a girl." He flung that at me as he stood up, and like a final exclamation point to the whole thing, he added, "My *error!*" and he ran back into the building as if he'd been shot out of a space capsule.

It only took a few seconds for me to get over being stunned. Then I felt the sting of hot tears in my eyes and the drops racing down my cheeks didn't cool off at all. And they kept coming.

The dumb tears were making the bread soggy on the other half of my dumb pot roast sandwich. I got up and dumped it, plus the brown paper bag and whatever was in it, in the trash can. I wondered if that superior male chauvinist had remembered to dump his litter where it was supposed to go. He'd probably let it fall from his pile of books and wherever it landed he'd blame some girl.

I turned toward the still-empty playground so I couldn't be seen wiping my face with my sleeves. I wished I could cut school for the rest of the day. Facing people and having to participate in class work seemed an overpowering ordeal. Some world problem solver, me. I couldn't put my mind on anything except the humiliating thing that just happened. Plus my total and irrevocable disappointment. I had thought up to about two minutes ago that he was a rare and exceptional person. Well, maybe it wasn't his fault that I'd pictured him as some kind of hero. He was only an ordinary mortal all the time. But I knew it was going to take me a while to get over the shock.

And then I remembered that my own personal troubles were still with me. No miracle by the name of Joshua Jackson had made them go away. I wondered if I would ever, ever be a well-adjusted, mature human being. Happiness was, of course, out of the question.

Later, in Spanish, when I watched Remi proudly telling some girls about her date with Gary Robinson, I thought it was lucky for me I didn't go public about my "boyfriend." Just as well he remained "only one of the other kids in the orchestra." Now Lucy would get a date and I'd be the one who had to ask a boy.

I practiced with a lot of heart that afternoon. I decided if I were trying out for the biggest symphony in the world, I'd have made it. If my selection were a funeral dirge, that is.

And my sadness was matched in degree only with my mother's elation when she came home and reported she had made a long-distance call and the New York School of Music would be happy to send out an application for her daughter's admission.

Maybe it wasn't such a bad idea. A change of environment might be just the thing I needed.

We had frozen TV dinners that night. Even if Sam had been there with one of his quiche Lorraine's or bouillabaisse's, it wouldn't have tasted any better. But regardless, I never missed Sam more. On a silver platter I could have handed him another problem to incubate.

11 Mom got the application the following Monday and her emotional state when she was reading it over and filling it out was something worth recording on film. But two days later I wasn't yet in the mood to cavort around the house snapping candid camera shots. It might have rubbed her the wrong way anyhow.

"Hey, Mom, don't look up—this is one of you, ecstatic over question number four—'How long since applicant has evidenced signs of genius?' "

I wouldn't go for that myself. One week earlier at exactly 11:34 A.M. I proved to me and the clarinet player what a genius I am. Clarinet player—I suppose I should say, opera star. Or rat. Or rat fink. Rat fink male pig. That's it. That's the whole description.

"Gina, they want to know, is your interest primarily performing, conducting, or composing?"

Burying myself alive, is what.

"Oh—uh—performing, Mom. You know that, per—forming." The end of the word really went downhill, fresh out of steam.

Mom wanted me to be a successful concert artist so much she was even asking questions she knew the answers to. Just saying them out loud must have made it seem more certain to her that it would happen.

She got lost again in the pile of papers, with the look of someone getting a holy blessing that was going to shield her from all danger, sickness, and harm for the rest of her life. My mother was at peace.

Which, of course, was not me. Peace was about as far from me as east is from west, winter is from summer, oranges from broccoli, and the piano from the clarinet.

A week ago I was ready to go to New York for keeps. But now, even though nothing was changed in my everyday life, I wasn't sure. I didn't know which way to think. Ought-to-think and actual feeling were mixed up. Near the surface I was telling myself that leaving here and starting fresh, with a new scene, new people was what I wanted. But down deep, the feeling me—that was something else. If I tell my mother I am happy to go, I won't be honest with myself. If I tell myself I want to go, it's only for an escape—to protect myself from living through an uncomfortable situation.

Well, I've got to be one hundred percent honest with her *and* with myself. I don't want to leave. Even though Joshua . . . but I don't want to leave.

There she was poring over that questionnaire, ready to sell her business, the house—my house . . . I had to tell her now! I got up from where I was sitting.

"Gina," a very weak Gina came out of her throat. "Gina," she said it again with the same weakness to it.

I looked over to her. "Mom?"

She didn't answer.

"Mom?" I repeated and sort of froze, looking across the room. She still didn't speak and I knew something was very wrong.

"Mom!" I said it again insistently, getting scared. I swooped over and stood beside her chair. "Are you all right?"

"Oh, I don't know," she said, rubbing her hand over her forehead. I thought sure she was sick—having an attack of some kind. I wasn't used to sudden attacks because Mom has always been Mrs. Healthy America. I mean if they ever had contests for that, she'd win by a mile. A cold now and then, anything else, never. So I got very funny flip-flops around my heart.

"Wh—where does it hurt?" I asked just as if I could do anything about it when she'd tell me. Call an ambulance, maybe. After all, I could hardly drive her to the Brookside General Hospital at twelve years of age.

She put her hand down on her desk, raised the most mournful face I've ever seen on her, and said in a voice that sounded like an echo, "The New York School of Music just threw us an underhanded curve."

"What do you mean, Mom?" I felt a little relief—she wasn't dying, at least.

"Question number sixteen. That's the curve. Not a question, a statement. It says, Gina, that if you are not a resident of New York City for one year prior to admission, the tuition fee is one thousand dollars."

The very first thing I felt was sorry for Mom. As if she were the one who wanted to get in to that school. Poor Mom. She'll probably want to take in washing at night to get the money. I couldn't let her hope for that. I had to hurry and tell her that NO WAY was I going.

"Mom, you know what Aunt Alice always says."

"Aunt Alice? What's she got to do with this?"

"Mom, Aunt Alice always says, 'Everything happens for the best.' "

She gave me a look to match the hollow tone in her voice. "Sure Aunt Alice can say that, but she doesn't have a daughter who qualifies for a music school."

"Mom, honest, Mom, it is for the best, Mom. Because—because I don't want to go."

Her face got full of warmth and tenderness. "What a sweetheart you are. You're just saying that to make me feel better, but I know how much you do want to go. And somehow, we'll get that tuition money, don't you worry, baby."

I had to make her believe me. "No, Mom, you can't!"

"I'll find a way, sweetheart, don't you worry," she said again.

"Mom, I—we—Mom, honest I don't want to

go. I never wanted to go. I'm not sacrificing anything, I just don't want to leave HERE."

I'm sure I never saw anyone's face change to so many different expressions in less than five minutes. From ecstasy to pain to love to bewilderment. I could understand them all, especially the bewilderment. She'd been concentrating so hard on what she thought was best for me that she figured I had to feel the same way too. And that was only half of what she was in for. She still had in store the great news about what I'd been doing Tuesday and Thursday afternoons. What I was about to divulge was worse than a mercy killing. It was like perpetual torture. She'd be finding out something that was going to hurt then and forever. She'd never feel she could have any faith in me for the rest of her life. I knew I'd heard that before. Sure did. Only a week earlier those were the words I'd used to try to convince Joshua he should live up to his obligations.

"Gina, why didn't you tell me?" In a voice from very faraway Mom brought me back to some courage and honesty that I was going to have to show.

"I—I guess I didn't try enough," I answered truthfully.

Mom was looking at me very hard. Then it seemed as if her gaze went past me even though she didn't take her eyes off my face.

I'd better tell her the rest of it. "There's

something else, Mom." I could hardly hear my words. "I haven't been practicing four hours every day." It was strange but I had thought once I got started it would be easy to spit it all out, one-two-three and it would be over with. But I was finding it very difficult.

"Why not, Gina?"

It sounded like an invitation to run over and hug her and get myself reassured and consoled. But I didn't because I figured that must be just in my mind. She can't be taking it like that. So I went ahead telling her more.

"Because there are after-school activities that I want to do as much as I want to play the piano. Is that—a terrible thing, Mom?"

My mother still hadn't taken her eyes off mine and now I could see tears rolling down her face. Only one thing I could think of—she must be so ashamed of me and so disappointed she probably never wants to see me again as long as . . .

"Gina," She stood up and was holding her arms out to me. This time there was no mistake. She *was* inviting me to get hugged and comforted. I took her up on it too.

12 Not twenty-five minutes after that our doorbell rang. Which, of course, didn't give Mom and me too much time to talk about a lot of stuff that had gone unspoken up to then. Of all the things we did get to say though, one more than any other stood out as unusual. It was as if it were me and Sam talking together. A couple of times, like lightning zooming through my head, I thought I knew why. Why it hadn't been that way before, I mean. It was on account of me taking for granted what wasn't supposed to be for granted at all. Had I ever given Mom a chance to yell or say no? No. I just kept quiet and suffered inside, making wrong conclusions about what she'd say *if*.

I bet that's the reason lots of grown-ups have problems—lack of communication so misunderstandings come up. I'm going to try to remember that so I won't make those kinds of mistakes later. I wonder, though, if keeping it in mind now makes any difference for the future. I don't know.

Anyway, some of the things we talked about before the bell rang were:

the orchestra;

"Honey, I'm *proud* of you. What did you think I'd be?"

other after-school activities;

"That depends. Piano has first priority, don't you agree?"

"Of course, Mom." I was glad I meant it because if I didn't, I'd have to tell her the truth, now that the ice was broken, and that particular truth might shatter her.

"You have to practice a *certain* amount each day." She sounded as if she were making concessions.

"I want to! Should I ask Mr. Sabbatini to reconsider the amount?"

"Nothing of the kind. I'll make that decision."

I had to smile. Mom was back to normal.

"You list all the after-school events you want to sign up for," she continued, "and we'll do some adding and subtracting on our own and see how it comes out."

and Joshua;

". . . and then he ran back in to the building, Mom, and I haven't seen or heard from him since."

She didn't give me a fast answer to that one.

"You know what," she said, and you could tell she'd given it a good deal of consideration, "I'd say you sounded like an old lady expecting him to buy that line."

I laughed out loud.

"Sure. You know who you remind me of?"

I knew and my face told her I did.

"Listen, that kind of talk is OK for your mother or anybody's mother, but so far as you're concerned, I'm afraid you let him down. That boy was counting on you to back him up and you let him down."

My smile faded.

"It's not the end of the world, sweetheart. I guarantee you that the next time you see him you'll know exactly how to handle it."

That was when the bell rang.

Believe me, my heart stopped. I mean when you've been talking about someone and a bell rings, your first thought naturally is that the person being talked about will appear.

Mom and I hesitated because we both must have had the same idea. Then we both started for the door at the same time. And then we both stopped.

"Tell you what," she said, "you answer and I'll stand behind you. And depending, I'll go upstairs and write some letters."

I took time out to give her a quick kiss and then I opened the door.

It was Sam. Sam, holding his suitcase and looking as if he'd just heard the first robin of spring.

Not that I wasn't glad to see him, but this was, I suppose you'd say, unexpected. In fact, Mom and I were so taken aback we stood there, one behind the other, just looking for a few seconds. Sam raised his eyebrows in surprise.

"You're not going to ask me in? It isn't as if I don't live here, you know." His eyes were twinkling.

"Sam, you've come back!" I reached out to hug him.

"Let the man put his bag down, Gina, and find out what's he's selling."

Mom didn't want him to think she was so ready to let him back in if he had come to stay. After all, only a few days before they'd had a fight and it didn't sound to me as if they parted on any good terms.

"Whatever happened to your country inn? Did it get too cold up country?" she asked sarcastically.

"Not too cold, Evelyn. Too dull. I'm a city boy and I've had an offer down here that I couldn't refuse."

"Such as?"

Sam looked at me, grinning and winked. "I came to be closer to my granddaughter."

He wasn't going to tell her I'd confided in him and not her! He couldn't tell her that now. Mom and I had the beginning of a good thing going. Sam wouldn't say anything to spoil it.

"The School Department has asked me to be on their staff." He said that without making it a joke.

"Sam!" I should *know* he wouldn't let on.

"Doing what?" Mom asked him, getting down to specifics.

"The junior and senior high schools want me to teach two courses—basic and gourmet cooking. I'm going to give it a whirl."

"Sam, then I'll get to see you in school!"

"Sure thing." He carried his bag to the staircase and put it on the third step blocking any passageway. He stood on the second step and dug his hands in his pockets, looking at us as we stood in front of him at the foot of the stairs.

"As to what I'm selling, Evelyn, it's a proposition."

He looked very seriously at Mom. She waited for him to talk while she gave him her full attention. It wasn't like the stare contests they have sometimes. It was as if they both wished the other day never happened and they wanted to start fresh.

"If you two can be flexible about it, I'd like to have sixteen Meadow Street as—well, my second home."

"You mean use this address as your headquarters as you go from job to job?"

"I mean, use it until I find a one-room efficiency apartment and come here as a visitor."

If he does that, I thought, he'll not only be moving out of our house, but he'll probably be moving in and out of our lives all the time. I tested that prospect on myself. If any problems came up he'd be out of town or just not available. Then what would I do? I was so used to expecting everyone else to solve my problems for me, I forgot that I finally scraped up some courage and used it. I was so in the habit of putting my burdens on Sam, I didn't know I could think and act for myself. Actually not too much time had passed since Sam had gone up to Charlie's, but the talk Mom and I had made things a little different than they used to be. It was still very important and beautiful between Sam and me, but a shade different. I guess, then, I'd be able to adjust to his leaving.

"Why do you want a one-room efficiency again, Sam?" Mom was asking.

"For the same reason I wanted it before. I'm an independent guy. Now let's talk about the other matter on my mind. It's Gina."

Since Sam was standing right in front of me and I cared about what he was saying, I hadn't taken my eyes off him. But after his last sentence, it was like a reflex action on my eyelids, and I was looking somewhere around the cuffs of his chinos. I felt so sorry for him. It was the same kind of sorry I had for Mom, before, when she found out about the thousand-dollar tuition that excluded me from going to the school she'd put her heart on. Now Sam was ready to talk about his solution to my problem—the one that he said he wanted to incubate in his head for a while. But he was too late. Mom and I had worked it all out and he was cheated out of feeling he'd helped me. I just wanted to die.

"Sam, we don't have to talk about Gina."

Oh Lord, Mom was making it worse. That was like rubbing it in.

"Why not?" Sam gave her a disturbed look.

"Well, for heaven's sake, Sam Parker, you gave

me a piece of your mind the other day and I thought it over, that's all. You were one hundred percent right. You convinced me and I hope I convinced Gina. Right, Gina?"

It was my mother's guileless face I was looking into then. Telling him that and making him believe it! Mom, you're as nice as your father any day.

"I'm convinced." I took in both of them.

"There really is no point rushing pell-mell into anything as big as a baby grand. Gina, next Saturday, how about we go looking for a good, first-hand upright?

"Sounds swell, Mom."

Sam didn't offer any objections, so I guess it sounded swell to him too.

Seven o'clock next morning, I could smell the bacon from my bedroom and on the way downstairs I could smell biscuits in the oven.

"Sam, those lucky kids who will take your courses—you'll make the whole town into French chefs."

"Flatterer. You love me just for my cooking, I can tell."

"Naturally." On tiptoe I kissed him on his cheek.

"You had a good talk with your mother?"

"Yes, Sam."

I could see a nice, satisfying expression as he

broke a couple of eggs in a bowl. "I thought it might work out that way. Now how would you like your eggs?"

I wasn't too sure if Mom had pulled the wool over his eyes at that. But it didn't matter. "Sunny-side up, Sam, if you don't mind."

"Don't mind at all."

The biscuits were golden. "Get me the bread basket and I'll have it ready in a jiff." Sam put a pat of butter in the frying pan and gently tipped the eggs into the sizzle.

I was on my second biscuit when I realized that when I talked things over with Mom, subtlety wasn't the method I'd used. I was more honest and straightforward than anything else. It was late in coming, and it wasn't the way Sam thought it should be done, but it was the natural way for me and it worked. I think maybe adults don't neces-sarily have the answers to everything. The love they feel for you is probably all you need—then you have to make it on your own.

On the corner of Country Road I had to wait for Remi and Lucy. They were so slow.

"Hi, Jody."

"Hi, Gina."

"Hi, Karen."

"Hi, Gina."

About five hi's later, Remi and Lucy showed up.

"You got a date! I can tell, Gina Barlow, by the

expression on your face that you got asked to the Thanksgiving Dance!"

That was a subject I'd just as soon nobody brought up.

"Why didn't you call us?"

"Why didn't you *tell* us?"

"I hate to disappoint you, but the expression on my face has nothing to do with dates. But the best thing happened."

"You mean the next best thing—second to dates," Remi, naturally.

"Well, I don't know about that." I was ready to accept the fact that dates and me would start happening when I was fifty years old.

"Well, what?"

"Well, Sam came back," I said, deciding I'd build up gradually to my new freedom. I knew way down deep that the reason I felt so really free hadn't much to do with four hours daily practice. It was that I'd been able to scrape up that courage to talk to Mom so I wasn't a slave to being afraid like I used to be.

"No offense, Gina, but is that all that caused that expression on your face?"

"I finally got the guts to talk to my mother and she . . ."

"Gina, how fantastic!"

"You'll be able to have more free time!"

Only half a sentence was all I had to say and they knew. I'd sure missed a lot by not being frank with them all this time. I wished I could talk to them about Joshua. But for me to do that, it had to be kind of—success talk. Only with my mother did I feel I'd talk about any failures.

And then I saw him.

I was standing in the hall in front of the bulletin board that had all the sign-ups. I was so excited over the prospect, I was going crazy over which ones to choose. I'd take anything! Ceramics, Creative Poetry, Anthropology, You and Your Environment.

"Hello, Gina."

It was such a low whisper it didn't reach my consciousness at first and when I heard it more plainly, I was aware it had been said twice. I turned. He looked awful. Not physically sick, mind you, but even if you didn't know him you'd say something was wrong. The look in his eyes, maybe. If he'd have been a grown man, you'd say he looked like he needed a shave.

"Hello." All of a sudden my voice was a whisper too.

Then we just looked at each other, neither saying anything, waiting for some encouragement. Time must have given it to him because there was nothing that I did.

"I guess that was a pretty stupid way for me to act the other day. Disappearing, I mean."

"Well, I was kind of—stupid myself."

Nobody seemed to get any encouragement

from that to move the conversation from there and we just looked at each other in silence again.

"The reason I did it," he was examining his shoes and then got back to my face. "I—my feelings got hurt. I thought you were trying to tell me you wouldn't go with me to the dance if I could go."

"No, that's not right," I said, not explaining further.

"You mean you would?"

It was as if the sun came into the building and warmed me all over. I smiled at him and said, "Sure."

He suddenly looked considerably better. Then bleak, again. "I wish—I wish I could ask you, but I have to perform the night of the dance."

"So you said the other day." Maybe my mother's words did convince him. I was glad he made the right choice.

"Well, I've been having a sort of discussion with my mother and . . ."

I wondered if his discussion was anything like mine.

"Well, Gina," he seemed to be getting his second wind, "I told her point-blank about wanting to ask you and she came up with another suggestion. She said to ask you to come with us to New York for the performance and you could stay at my uncle's too. Do you want to? Do you think your mother will say it's OK?"

I felt so good, I was basking in it. Joshua was

my friend again. Then, just like my mother said I would, I knew exactly how to handle it. I grinned and said, YES.

I could hardly wait to see Remi and Lucy. I had some success talk I could share with them—easy.

Aunt Alice was right all the time.

About the Author

Julia First grew up, went to school, and worked in the Boston, Massachusetts, area. She still lives nearby, in Newton Highlands, a suburb of Boston, with her husband, Melvin.

When Julia First decided to become a writer, she began with typical eagerness and was given an instantly warm reception by readers. *Move Over, Beethoven* is her fifth novel to be published in four years.

DATE			
DEC. 1 5 1988			
NOV 1 7 1989			